A Small Harvest
of Pretty Days

Larry Kimport

Foremost Press
Cedarburg, Wisconsin

Also by Larry Kimport

In the Kingdom of the Wilderness

Larry Kimport
Lumberton, New Jersey

Published by Foremost Press

ISBN-10: 0-9789704-4-6
ISBN-13: 978-0-9789704-4-4

This is a work of fiction. Any similarity of characters or events to real persons or actual events is coincidental.

For Mary Vin, my loving wife

"I says to myself, there ain't no telling
but I might come to be a
murderer myself yet . . ."

~ ~ ~ Huckleberry Finn

"So the word became flesh
and resided among us . . ."

~ ~ ~ John 1:14

CHAPTER 1

The first time I ever saw him he frightened me, oh so, the way he appeared out of nowhere, distant and faint through the frozen white of that January morning. He moved straight and tall through that bitter cold, toward me, but still far out upon the ice of the river, like he had risen up and out of the frozen Susquehanna herself. You see, at the time, he could have been my savior or my killer, as he strode, still distant and silent to me where I was hid.

I, myself, stayed crouched and huddled, hiding within the dark hollow of this long since fallen tree I scrambled into. And I watched him, through the frosty mists of my own breathing, as he closed toward me in my hiding place, and toward my other two problems that were somewhere else in those woods that cold, scary morning.

And as I listened for, and stayed hid from that Mr. Horace Wills and his scary friend, I watched the man on the river through a knothole against my shoulder. He was still a good ways off, beneath a tilted big brimmed hat. He looked to be wrapped tight in a straight coat and cape. He also carried a cane or a walking stick that struck silently upon the ice to the cadence of his frosty breaths and steady stride.

You see, I was awfully frightened that cold winter morning, all alone save myself, amongst those riverbank trees, with two men behind me, and another before me.

CHAPTER 2

I was returning home that early morning, to Montoursville, a good ride downriver from Williamsport, where I had spent the better part of the week tending to Mrs. Deacon's ailing aunt, Mrs. Snyder. I still thank the angels that my little Emma wasn't with me. Mrs. Deacon, you see, was my employer at the time, and had been upwards of seven years. She and Mr. Deacon had taken Emma and me in when Emma was but three. I was their maid of sorts, their house-girl, but more about that by and by.

That morning I rounded the wooded Sand Hill section of road on one of the Deacons' older bays, when an hour or so past sunup, and just west of the Loyalsock Creek, I come upon none other than Horace Wills, riding alongside a man on a mule, a big stupid looking soul. Across the cold distance I figured them strangers, but as we neared one another, Horace's wild red hair and homely face did slowly come to me. And I began to fear some to his slow riding presence, and to that face of his, with his harelip, so peculiar, unlike any other. He had also aged a good deal, but so had I, I suppose. It'd been nearly three years since I last saw him, and that was at a distance. And of course over eleven years had passed since that one awful time of mine. Now here we were, he and I, all alone, save that brutish looking man riding with him on our frozen road to Montoursville.

Well, the three of us come upon one another, with quiet nods. I believed that he and his friend had been drinking. They looked so, and anyway I could smell it in the stillness of that frozen air of just after dawn.

I tried to keep my face down, but Horace Wills recognized me. "Well, look who it is, out here all alone in this cold," his harelip smiled.

Then he pulled up his horse, leaned a bit and said, "Clara Waltz, it's been a long time."

"Good morning, sir," I greeted him as best I could, not saying a word to his friend on the mule as I rode on, never pausing the Deacons' old bay.

Then Horace spoke again, from behind me, but I paid him no mind, at least not out loud as I feared being alone with the two of them. My thoughts ran though, as I prayed the distance between us would grow. For some reason my mind swam with Mr. Horace Wills, his barroom and little hotel up in Williamsport, then that stretch of time when he was gone, off traveling somewhere with the circus, before returning to struggle, as they say, with a little show of his own that he traveled with as far south as Sunbury, and up as far north as Elmira and as west as Lock Haven. You see, he and some other men, five in all, two mere children, like myself back then, took their way with me one night all those years ago. From it, life gave me little Emma, just as it gave to me, then took from me, little Ellie, her sister, some sad days later. You see, they were born as twins.

But back to that quiet, frozen road. Mr. Wills called out to me again after a couple of hundred yards had gone between us. I heard laughter as well, followed by more comments. I tried to pay them no mind, but oh me oh my, when I turned and saw old Horace turn his own horse about, I dug the bay hard in her ribs, prompting her into a gallop, hard, toward Montoursville, trusting her not to fall upon the frozen road as she blew her frosty breaths. But when I looked back, hoping to be alone, I saw Mr. Wills was riding hard too, with that big man on his mule not far behind.

The old bay's stride sounded out loud upon the planks of the bridge crossing the Loyalsock Creek. Filling with fear, I teared up, with them same tears to freeze just as quickly upon my cheeks in the wind of the ride. Across the bridge, I turned her hard right, downstream, to head for the aloneness of the canals and the river. I don't rightly understand why I took this direction, but I did it. I suppose I just didn't want any of those men, and their ways, near my Emma, nor near the nice Deacons who allowed their home to be ours as well. Anyway, shortly I crossed the railroad tracks, keeping the bay hard at it.

A ways past the tracks I pulled up on her, slowing her a bit, trying to gather my thoughts some, hoping Mr. Wills and his friend had given up on this business. I couldn't feel the cold then either as I worked at straightening my overdress, beneath my jacket and cape, while allowing the bay to walk through a stretch of farm fields and broken forest. Then with no one about, save myself, I heard Horace's whoop and a holler, with a distant lone gallop. I feared again, figuring they aimed to have quite a sport of me.

Digging into the old bay, I ran her again, just a bit, to the back of the fields. Then I worked her down into the forests that skirted the river, just above the canals.

In only half a mile or so, I felt her tiring beneath me within those trees. I dismounted the bay and listened. Then I walked her. Opposite the fields, the frozen river laid white and frozen before the rise of the mountain beyond. All was quiet, save for the frosty breathings and stick crackling clomping of the bay. Then I heard Mr. Wills again, off in the distance behind us, calling my name.

"Clara! Clara! I just wants to talk to you!"

I slapped at the bay, but she wouldn't trot off far. I heard another of his hollers, then a distant laugh. Near panicky, I cried for the bay to get so I could hide myself. Then I found a thick switch and lashed her good, to find her own way home. Near as quick, I half fell and stumbled down into the thicker riverbank trees.

Through the winter quiet, I thrashed my way through the debris of the great flood of the year before, the flood of '89 that broke the logging booms of Lock Haven and Williamsport, sending the cut timber and floodwaters south on the Susquehanna, destroying the bridges, factories and homes of Muncy, Montgomery, Milton and Selingsgrove and beyond. You see, the events of this cold morning were in January of 1890, when in my fear I fell and grasped and climbed my way about the debris not salvaged by the lumbering men, listening for Horace Wills, and for his scary friend, hearing one or the other once or twice.

In short time, I suppose minutes, I stumbled upon this hollowed out, fallen big tree and crawled in, backwards, collecting about me my overskirt and bustle as I went. Breathing too hard, and trying not to, I then found the knothole, through which I first saw that third man, the one out walking upon the frozen water.

* * *

I tried to calm some, saying short prayers to myself, but my heart leapt again as I heard Mr. Wills, closing through the trees. "Miss Waltz! Come on now, Clara, I seen you cut your horse loose!"

I looked out of the knothole. The man on the river moved through light wisps of blown up snow.

"I just wants to talk with you a bit!" Horace called out. "No need for all this runnin' and such!"

Then Horace called out again, several times, seeming to find his way nearer to my fallen tree as the man upon the river made his own way toward the both of us. It must have been only minutes, but it seemed forever before I finally saw Mr. Wills, still upon his horse. He was working her through the gnarled riverbank growth, blinking into and out of my line of sight through the bare trees. Then I heard his voice. "You can't hide in here forever, Clara."

I curled farther back into my woody darkness, trying to still my frosty breathing. Then I startled again. I may have gasped. Through the knothole I saw the third man, nearly upon the embankment, certain to rise just before my fallen tree.

The events to unfold next I can only guess to most of, so I'll relate only those that I saw through the larger opening before me, or through the knothole to my side.

Mr. Wills quieted, pulling up on his horse, I suspected upon seeing the man from the river, which come to be so because he asked in that direction, "Good morning, good man! Have you seen a young woman amongst these trees?"

The man replied something, but I couldn't make it out as he too came within my forward view. He was wrapped in a cape beneath his big brimmed hat. His cane was a thick, straight stick. He approached Mr. Wills, who remained in his saddle.

I watched hard at their figures, which were broken up by a scattering of thinner trees. They talked, but I couldn't make any of it out. Once or twice Horace Wills even laughed at this thinner man who appeared as old or even older than he. Then, to save my own soul, what I did see next was the man with the walking stick reach behind himself. And making as though he was scratching at his own back or something, he slowly withdrew a long knife from beneath his tattered cape. Then my own breath left me as I watched him, in a sudden slashing, rip open a God awful wound across Mr. Will's horse's throat. Oh, I swear my own breath did leave me.

I thought I saw the knife fly off as Mr. Will's horse reared up in terror. Horace himself fell from her as the red of the poor animal's blood appeared immediately. Then the two men fought so amongst the trees and the bare thicket, upon the frozen ground and into and out of my lines of sight. Horace's horse tried to whinny, I think, but made only horrid sounds as she thrashed heavily about, once running blindly into one of the larger trees, smearing its bark with her own blood as she left my vision.

I don't know which was worse, but the men's fighting scared me more. I don't know what I should have expected, but there were no words between them, only sounds and grunts and hard breathing and sticks snapping and branches whipping as they twice came into my sight, rolling and holding to one another, and crashing about in those woods. I heard Horace's horse, then I saw her again. This time her gait hobbled and leaned as more blood streamed from her flaring nostrils and working mouth. Then I heard the sound of ice breaking down at the river's edge, which I couldn't see. Then Horace's horse must have circled behind me once more, because she then struggled so, walking sideways, before my opening again, where she collapsed in my full view, dying upon that frozen ground with one big red bubble of breath stretching out from her one nostril.

And as I noticed the steam rising from Horace's horse, I became fearfully aware that all else was quiet too. Oh me oh my, how I feared for myself and my little Emma.

Then there was walking that I couldn't see, a slow, stick crackling, woodsy sound that frightfully appeared before me as that third man, the one from out upon the ice of the river. He approached the dead horse, and with his chest heaving he looked down at her. Then he leaned against a near tree, breathing hard, pushing out frosty breaths. I might have made a sound of my own, but he must not have heard it in my hiding. I took notice that his hands shook some. And his age showed too, perhaps of fifty to sixty years as he straightened his big brimmed hat. I held my breath then, staying as quiet as I could as I watched him look for, then find his knife. He wiped the long blade with shaking hands, and before I knew it, his lean figure then flickered slowly away amongst those quiet again, riverbank trees.

I stayed hid of course, and it wasn't long before I heard another man's voice, childlike but deep, calling out for Horace. I swear I couldn't feel the cold at all as Horace's large friend hobbled his way into my fearful view. He was dismounted, leading his mule through the riverbank brush straight ahead, before my large opening. And oh Lord, how I got a good look at him as I stilled my breathing once more. I saw his unshaven, swollen face and that heavy blanket which I took before to be an awkward cape. I heard him cussing his mule, and I nearly cried out, as he did, upon discovering Horace's dead horse.

He made an awful sound, not a word at all as he dropped his mule's rope reins and looked about, as fearful as myself I recall. Then he stilled himself, looking down toward the river's edge, then upstream, then toward my own fallen tree as I froze fast. Then he left my view. His heavy steps circled my fallen tree. Then they stilled. He called out, "Orace! Misser Orace!" in his deep voice.

My smaller knothole did me no good, but it'd be over shortly as his steps became those of heavy stumbling, up through the thicket behind me, to come before my larger hole and my tearful view once more. He looked stupid to me, and fearful and confused as he gathered up his rope reins, still making his sounds to none at all. He looked once more to Horace's steaming horse, but not at all toward the frozen riverbank. Then he too made his way off through the bare trees, trying to be quicker, falling twice. My knothole served me here, for I recall he began to cry as he tugged and jerked, and cussed at his mule.

* * *

I stayed hid for quite some time, and I truly can't say for just how long. But when I got up the resolve to crawl out of my woody darkness, Horace's horse was still steaming, but just barely so.

I looked about ever so quietly, then ventured to the river myself, and then, oh Lord, I saw Mr. Horace Wills himself. He laid down at the river's edge, as dead as his horse, stuck into a hole in the ice. And he appeared oddly uncomfortable, with his head and shoulders gone beneath the ice, with only his left arm bent back, up and out of the hole, dead and motionless, like his crossed legs. I suppose that was how he perished at the hands of that man, struggling to pull himself out, just to breathe at the end.

I feared calling for the bay, and figured her long gone anyway. I had to make something up, with her returning to the farm without me and all. Dogs would do. Spooked by dogs, I decided. I made my way up and out of those riverside trees, to cross the farmlands and the wooded fence rows, that laid silent and cold between the river and the railroad tracks and the town beyond.

I remember the cold coming back to me, and some quarter of the way I suddenly vomited, so fast it scared me. I was thinking at the time of how it seemed to be so much easier for that man to kill Horace's horse. Oh, how he struggled with Horace himself. There was no blood though, not with Mr. Wills, not that I saw. That man from the river must have, at the end, just let the river do it.

All alone, save myself, I started to weep as well. And oh, how I wept and had myself such a good crying. You see, it'd been a long time indeed since I had allowed myself such a good weeping. And there was a stray cow somewhere too, for I heard her lowing at one point, somewhere off in the cold, as though she was caught or something, and as all alone as me.

* * *

That night, after I had my little Emma asleep, tucked into our bed in our corner room, my reflections took me to poor little Ellie of so long ago, and of how she pained so in her brief time. Then I thought again of that morning's events, at the river's edge. This took me to turning up our lamp a quarter turn more than usual, to read of killing in my Bible. You see, I took to Jesus' counsel, and the Good Book in general, while still just a girl, sometime after that one night those eleven or so years before. And it was good for me too, taking up the good counsel.

Anyway, beneath our heaviest quilts, I came across several Scriptures, but only one that stayed with me to ponder. I found it in Numbers 35:16-18. Jehovah was going on to Moses upon the desert plains about the new laws of Israel. It went something like: "Now if it was an instrument of iron by which he could die he is a murderer . . . a small stone by which he could die . . . he is a murderer . . . if it was a small instrument of wood by which he could die . . . he is a murderer. Without fail the murderer should be put to death."

Well, I didn't see any such instruments, save that man's knife put to Horace's horse, and that flew off. I do recall watching him find it, though, to wipe it, and then sheathe it. But I thought more over why these things even have to happen, and then those thoughts became wonderings of who between those two fighting men was even the worse murderer.

In time, I turned down our lamp to the cold night outside. Then I snuffed it entirely and smelled deep of Emma's hair as I snuggled in with her. And I do believe I even tried to cry, for it somehow felt good earlier that day.

But I just couldn't do it. Not again. Not for the likes of Horace Wills.

CHAPTER 3

To more truly relate the events of that late winter, which all started with that icy killing, and of those that followed both gaily and darkly against the blossoming spring that followed, I must back up. I must do so to be as honest as I'm capable of being. First, my name, of course, is Clara Waltz, and my age was, when these events did happen, thirty years as of the autumn before.

To not wander with this, I was born some sixty miles north of our Susquehanna Valley, across the forested mountains, in Wellsboro, Pennsylvania. My father moved us, my mother, myself and my older sister, into our Cogan Station home, north of Williamsport when I was two, to remember that area as my only childhood home.

Cogan Station wasn't much more than a little railroad depot along the Northern Central Line, which ran northbound from Williamsport, up through Elmira, New York, via our stop, with others at Ralston and Troy. It's probably not much more than that today, and it might even be less. My mother passed away several years prior to these events I intend to relate. After mother died, my older sister married a Berwick man. They with their children still live down there along the North Branch of the Susquehanna. I've never been there. Back when these events did happen, my father, still living at the time, and still in Cogan Station, wouldn't take company with Emma and myself. I used to miss him, but then no more.

You see, the world was changing then, and oh so fast. Of course it still is, but it was different for us back then, for us so far from the great cities of New York and Philadelphia and Pittsburgh. Us far from the great names that I'd see news of in the *Gazette*, or overhear from the company of men who visited with Mr. Deacon, names like Edison, John Rockefeller, Carnegie and the Vanderbilts, places and names that I heard such talk of back then, as I served the Deacons and their guests such spreads of meals as we could put to a table.

And of course, there was my world. And I was pleased with it, my world of tending to the wash, the meals, busying myself about the nice smells of the Deacon pantry and the work of Mrs. Deacon's fine big kitchen. And as always, I suppose, the men and the women kept separate worlds, and, I suppose, as other proper domestic help, I too kept a third one, a much smaller one of mine and Emma's own, seeing after things, in servitude and in fairness.

Ours was about the rooms of that nice big house that needed to be kept after so. And the great stove in the kitchen, and the other in the parlor that Emma and I kept stoked from mid-October through late March, with all the coal and ashes that needed sifting and toted in and out. And of course the wash. There was always washing to attend to, from the men's soiled farming wash, right up to Mrs. Deacon's finest things, all crocheted or macramé. And the soapmaking too, for once every month I boiled down of a couple of dozen cakes for about the house and the farm in general.

But enough concerning my own little world back then. Mind you, with the lumbering we had our own greatness of sorts right there in our own valley, even proclaimed for a spell as the lumbering capital of the nation.

Back in the seasons of these events some even said Williamsport would regain her greatness, certain to happen, as others claimed that the mighty forests were razed and our city in that valley would tire on her laurels over time. Anyway, I'm certain I'll tell more of the stately mansions along Third and Fourth Streets, of the toils and songs of the large crews of men who felled the mighty trees, and of the wealth in general that flourished throughout that valley as the timber floated to the river, down the creeks of Pine Creek, Lycoming Creek and the Loyalsock, to gather in the mighty booms, to be collected and sorted, to be cut and sold. And oh me oh my, how I've gone and wandered with this reflection.

* * *

To commence most properly, I must tell of my ordeal of eleven years before that season of killing, when I was at an age to reflect and think over my future prospects, but instead chose to be a foolish girl. You see, I took to frequenting a barroom not far from my home, along the road north that led to Ralston, through Trout Run. This ordeal, you see, would shape itself into the very colors and shadows of my life ever since, and I suppose it began with Joseph Logan.

Joseph Logan grew up in a hollow off Lycoming Creek, downstream from my own home. And I tell you, did I ever have a soft spot in my heart for him ever since I was twelve or thirteen, just graduated out of that grammar school of ours. Nothing ever came of it of course, or nothing good, save my Emma. Anyway, at sixteen or seventeen himself, Joseph took to the circus life, with his brother, Charles, and that Mr. Horace Wills one time when the big show come around. Charles, who I little knew, had already been with the show seven or eight years by then, and would remain with it until the season of these events, long after Joseph would give that life up. Anyway, late in the summer of my eighteenth year, when their circus show was set to pull out of Williamsport by rail after a five-day stop, I ran into Joseph, among the others at the same barroom I related to earlier.

I will not spare myself with this. I shouldn't have been in such a place as that, me being still a child and all. And of course I drank too, of their liquors and ale, and oh how I still fancied Joseph, he at nineteen and all worldly with his travels and his tales. To be honest before the Lord, I did indeed consent to lay with him that night, out in that closed up supply shed. But I never, not ever, asked for, nor ever wanted in any way that swinging lantern that came in before the others, casting the evil shadows of their laughter that kept up through my struggle with the five of them in all.

And in the end all five did have at me, or take me in their way—one of them twice. I suppose that's why I couldn't cry for Horace Wills but once.

Anyway, the five were Joseph and his brother, Charles, Mr. Horace Wills and Mr. Stacy Kremer, the son of a farmer from Linden at the time, and, as I was to learn much later, the fifth was another circus man, a Mr. Rudolph Burr. As I hope a soul could imagine, my labor was about my conception, and for long after.

Joseph, in time, returned to Williamsport. Emma was four or so by then. By the time of our season of killing, he'd be living in Newberry, and married and all with children. I understood he worked in a sawmill. There must have been ten or fifteen or so still in operation at the time.

* * *

Well, I had the most terrible of times following that awful night. It was a time of confusion for me, a time when the days and the nights of the end of that summer and those of the beginning of that autumn blurred into one another. It was a time when I somehow became lost within myself, unable to properly confess my thoughts and feelings to the very few who'd listen to me in their own ways. You see, I did have a few female friends and acquaintances, but they too drifted off from me, I suppose just as those men and boys so easily did.

And I tried to tell my tale too, and shortly after that terrible night, but I was scorned as a whore as I couldn't even sort for myself between guilt and what may indeed invite such a thing. As I said, those blurry weeks that followed can only come back to me now as distant sad splashes of recall. I'll try again here, for this larger tale, but the order will never be correct, I'm sure.

I know I wept a great deal. I also recall throwing away my undergarments, a new whalebone bodice, and of course my knickerbocker drawers that had been torn from my bottom. I remember trying to repair and tidy them both up, after those men and boys left me in that shed, all alone, save my own trembling, drunken tears, without even that swinging lantern to dress myself by. It was a season of living with a silent judgment, while having to fear seeing at least one of them again. I wanted to do something terrible to them, and I didn't want to be touched and I feared any crowd of people. My own father, whom I tried to hide it all from, somehow heard of that business. He must have, for he ceased speaking to me some two weeks later.

Somewhere in that autumn I heard talk of myself inviting, even enjoying the whole ordeal, and in those same weeks my confusion turned to sorrow for this thing that, Lord be my witness, just wasn't my fault. And by the time the leaves began turning, for I do recall the reds and the oranges, I even pondered my own maidenness after being approached by a man and a woman from a brothel, by any other name, down along a riverfront street in Williamsport. The woman, at first kindly, assured me that some of the other girls also had children of their own, for you see, by then I was already swelling with child. Growing slowly with my children of Emma and Ellie.

As for my maidenness, I certainly was sad some, and it did hurt a bit, but I suppose that may matter more for men. Of course I remained without men, in that way, until the summer that followed the winter of the killings, which started that early morning at the Susquehanna's edge.

* * *

I lived quietly with my silent father across that winter, friendless, save the Good Book that I slowly embraced. By early December I began attending Sunday worship up Lycoming Creek. The kindly Pastor English welcomed me into his services through his silent acknowledgement of my presence. His congregation of our neighbors grew accustomed, I suppose, to my attendance, but remained distant nevertheless to me and my circumstances. None, of course, knew of my receiving a letter from my one attacker, Stacy Kremer. In that single correspondence he pleaded:

". . . please, please forgive me,
Miss Waltz. I meant only to be playing
cards that night. It is urgent for me

to have you understand that I am not
an evil man, but moreoever . . .”

and then his letter most shocked me with:

“. . . I am the promising son of a
proper Linden farmer, Miss Waltz,
and I would make for a proper suitor
if you would allow me to court you, if
you could find it in your . . .”

Of course I never responded. He was a criminal to me. I
swear I did see him though, two times about our Cogan Station
area.

Anyway, it was sometime that winter that I did change in
how I viewed my circumstances and myself. You see, my Bible
became my solace as I, in time, came to fancy myself as a widow
of sorts. You see, just as with a widow's plight, I didn't ask for
what had happened to me. My own foolishness could have brought
me the children I was carrying, but not the scorn and the hu-
miliation that accompanied my loneliness everywhere. To comfort
me and guide me, I found in 1 Timothy, where Paul spoke to
Timothy, that genuine child of faith, 5:3, “Honor widows who
are actually widows,” and 5:4, “But if any widow has children or
grandchildren, let these learn first to practice Godly devotion to
their own households . . .” Then in 5:6, “But the widow who
goes in for sensual gratification is dead though she is living.”
And in 5:8, “Certainly if anyone does not provide for those who
are his own . . . he has disowned the faith . . .”

You see, I had to find a path for myself, and I could see one
here where Paul went on, from 5:11 to 13, about widows and
their sexual tendencies, and how they could get gossipy and
meddlesome and unoccupied in general. I knew I could be some
of those things mentioned, but I also yearned in my lonesomeness to resist the undesirable others, for I especially quieted myself
to 5:14, “Therefore, I desire the younger widows to marry, to

bear children, to manage a household . . ." You see, these Scriptures whispered to me about forgiveness and a new start somehow. I just needed a path from my storm.

And of course I also grew in my motherly way. Such a strange aloneness it was, bringing someone else into it as I swelled with child in my aloneness at my Sunday worships, about my father's house, and while attending to household errands my father never acknowledged. And into that warming spring, my aloneness and swelling continued amongst those beautiful hills and mountains of my girlhood home, and by the first of May, my sister kindly journeyed up from her own home in Berwick to be with me for the birthing of my babies. She brought her eldest of two. This was the first I had seen of my little niece.

Then in mid-May I began to labor one warm evening, and by chilly morning, a midwife from up in Steam Valley was at my side with my sister. And with a light frost upon the ground outside, and with my father gone off to somewhere for the duration, I pained and cried my way through the first, then worked more easily through the second. Both of them girls, Ellie and Emma.

Then the darkness descended once again upon that time of my life, to carry on as such for my memory. And once again I can only relate certain images and feelings of those days that followed, and once more certainly not in any proper order.

Both of my babies at first took healthy to my bosom, but then, oh, the third or fourth day I suppose, little Ellie ceased suckling.

For our efforts the midwife returned and wet-nursed her, but to no proper end. And then came that slow sorrow, for Ellie found it difficult to breathe through her clear nose, and a day later her tiny lips and nose blued over from her weakening heart. The doctor came and speculated Infant Blood Infection. A fever then swept through her as her little belly swelled and her skin paled further. She grew sleepy and vomited, but I failed to see how, for she hardly ate, from myself or from the midwife in her brief time. Her little messes yellowed through, and then the saddest of my days came the day she took to little fits, the same day her little life stilled forever.

I was held and comforted by my sister and the midwife. I was reminded that I had sisters of sorts in that regard. Not far up the creek, Laura Wellington lost two of her seven. My own mother, her first I learned. Even Pastor English's good wife lost at least one. But these did me little good for mine was a different unfairness. You see, it was my conception that was so painful to I who could bear it. In my mind the babies were to be left unharmed, and I silently questioned if my little Emma was to become my burden or a solace, for I just didn't know. But of course across her years, she became nothing but blessings, never a yoke about my shoulders, but a lone kiss to my life that sorely needed one. Indeed, she became the part of my life left better as her poor sister was cursed to a pillar of salt to my own Sodom and Gomorrah.

* * *

But oh me oh my, back to that winter of 1890, back to the Deacons' fine home amidst their wintry farm in the beginning of that season of killing. I suppose witnessing that icy murdering prodded me into thinking all over again; being of course that it was Mr. Horace Wills that got killed. And I pitied myself over how I had to endure, until I found in Judges 19:22-29, this story about this fearful traveling man who holed up with his concubine in a stranger's house, being surrounded by evil men who desired the man himself. In his fear he tried to offer the virgin daughter of the homeowner, but it was his concubine whom he eventually sacrificed. In any event, after the evil men had their ways with her, she was found unconscious the following dawn, only to be taken home to be cut into twelve pieces, to be spread about every territory of Israel. The Scripture stated that she had died prior to her butchering, but I wondered that winter night, what if the girl had survived? How would she have endured? And of course I gave thanks in prayer that my lot wasn't as horrid as hers.

Nevertheless, with my new burden of having witnessed a killing, I pitied myself for having no true company in life, save my Emma and my own lonely thoughts. But I could have, I must relate, for by that winter Stacy Kremer had approached me with his intentions two more times, each three or four years apart. By the second of his offerings, he boasted having left his father's farm, having bought one himself somewhere along the line between Muncy and Montgomery, just below where the river turns hard south, on the other side of the mountain from me, thank goodness.

But I did have the Deacons, especially Mrs. Deacon, or Elizabeth, as she insisted I call her, which I would at times, but never before company, and they kept a lot of company. Her husband, Mr. Henry Deacon, was quite prosperous, you see. He was something of a gentleman farmer, owning a great deal of land. We lived on the home farm, they called it, which his hired men farmed right there at the edge of Montoursville. And he owned more land which he leased out for timber rights up the Loyalsock Creek and some other places unknown to me. As I said before, I was of domestic employ, and Mr. Deacon was a man of business, of which I knew nothing. But back to my world of loneliness, the Deacons were blessed with three children, and that did help. Their eldest was Sarah, who turned ten that winter, nearly a year behind my Emma, but of course of another station in life. Their son, Joshua was but seven, and a rascal. And Ellen was their infant. I came to be acquainted with, and employed by this fine family through the thoughtful efforts of Pastor English back up in Cogan Station, for he was friends with the Reverend John Ashhurst there in Montoursville, of the Deacons' church up in town on Loyalsock Avenue. I knew Pastor English at least acknowledged me back then, but I didn't know that he worked on an answer to my problem. He was a good man for this. I remained lonely, but I was indeed thankful for Emma and I to have what home we had within Mr. and Mrs. Deacon's own.

But to be true to this, after that riverbank killing I felt alone all over again, for of course it was Horace Wills who was killed.

Sometimes I couldn't rid those thoughts and images from my mind, both those of the murdering and those of all those years before. And then other times I'd ponder quite intentionally over what I had seen from within that log. I thought about death, then read of it from my Bible. Then I found wisdoms regarding fear and anger, and I studied those, I suppose regarding my own, as well as what might have been that man's, who came from across the frozen river several weeks before. I recall finding something in the Proverbs of Solomon, son of David, about being slow to anger, and impatience and foolishness. But I especially remember Proverbs 22:24-25, which read: "Do not have companionship with anyone given to anger, and with a man given to fits of rage you must not enter in, that you may not get familiar with his paths . . ." For you see, I didn't know it then, but another fearful thing was laying for me just about that time.

* * *

It was late February, near a month since that riverside killing, when Mr. Benjamin Mason and his wife, Sarah, came down from Williamsport to dine with the Deacons. The two men were longtime business associates, and often enjoyed meeting as such on Sundays. The Masons came, as most of the Deacons' guests did, taking the afternoon train on the Catawissa Branch. There was also a good long stretch of conversation to overhear while tending to the two men while preparing their dinner as well.

As was usual, I could listen in on a good deal of opinion, some quarrel and an awful lot of convincing. Although friends, the two men disagreed on a good deal.

"It's no time to panic, Henry. These things run in cycles," declared Mr. Mason, from Mr. Deacon's own chair. "Cycles that take years, not seasons."

Mr. Deacon was fast. "The Populists took eight state legislatures last November, Ben, and the mere mentioning of Mary Clemons Lease boils my blood," he answered as he cleaned his pipe, as I myself became aware of someone moving about outside on the porch.

I had sent Emma out back to shake out the big tablecloth, so I stole a look from where I was, in the parlor, and oh my Lord was I nearly struck down, for I knew it was him.

I didn't have to look hard, or study him, or anything as my own heart startled, pounding away with first, the whereabouts of my Emma, and then the full weight of the knowledge of Horace Wills' killer being upon the farm, just through that window, so near to me again.

Those moments of first seeing him again come to me now as a blur, because that's how they happened to me then. My breath left me. The men talked on. One of them laughed. Emma must have come in through the back, because I heard her asking something of someone in the kitchen. I tried to calm myself with that knowledge, as I looked toward, then away from the passing shadows of that man, busying himself about something upon the porch.

I purposely tried to pick up on the conversations in the parlor and in the kitchen, trying hard to settle myself, listening not for their words, but for anyone's awareness of my new fears.

There were none. I moved away from the windows, alone with my knowledge of that killing man. I tried to speak to Mr. Mason, to say anything at all, but Mr. Deacon was quicker, with concerns of his own.

"No, Ben, I only hired one, to work the home farm here. I'm not pleased with the wintering of the stock. Not at all."

Mr. Mason answered him with something I can't recall, but save me, in moments more Mr. Deacon answered Mr. Mason with, "Hired him three days ago. Seems to be a quiet fellow."

And as I was clearing Mr. Mason's tea table, trying to not shake, I was took with, "In fact, Ben, the new man's upon the front veranda as we speak."

CHAPTER 4

Across the following days I watched for him, hoping he'd never set foot in the big house. I saw him afar, and I watched from near. Oh me oh my, it was him and his tall slenderness, and his kindly, quiet-looking killer's face of handsomeness, in spite of his age, and in spite of the bones of his cheeks that stuck out so. I watched his face as he talked with others, but I had yet to hear his voice that rose up from that bobbing Adam's apple, a voice that everyone so seemed to enjoy. Apparently he was a Southerner, and spoke with a modest drawl.

Those early days were strange ones, still in the cold of that waning winter. For it seemed to be just he and I and our secret that he didn't know we shared. It was a fearful and lonely intimacy to have with another soul. I prayed for guidance and read from my Bible, finding in Mark 11:24, where Jesus had busted up the Temple for all the business going on, where He spoke to Peter, "This is why I tell you, all the things you pray and ask for have faith that you have practically received, and you will have them." Oh me oh my, how I worried if my own evil thoughts brought on this cruel time, or if His words went beyond, meaning to return me to the peace of my duties and responsibilities about my Emma and the Deacons.

I can recall quietly climbing into the heavy blankets of mine and Emma's bed in the nights of those first weeks, where I'd lay awake, silently trying to place this man whose name I came to learn was Finley, a Mr. Hank Finley. I wondered about his past, and where he might have come from. Drifters were all over, especially with the lumbering slowing as it was. But I couldn't place him amongst those strong men of the forests. The tobacco and the whiskey I could believe, but not the sunup to sundown laboring, year round amongst the heaviest of the timbers. These ponderings were on my mind too many nights, well after I'd turn down our lard oil lantern, when I should have been tending to the comfort of my sleeping child.

By February's end I managed to get Emma and myself off to Ellie's grave, up Trout Run. And I also learned, about my duties and while eavesdropping, that Mr. Finley earned a good wage of $8.50 per week for his sixty hours, give or take. And by the first week of March, Mr. Finley and I first spoke to one another, over laundered work clothes I fell behind on. And I found it strange and odd that he deferred to me as "ma'am," considering my fearing him and all, and with my being twenty years or more his junior.

Later that same week the Reverend Ashhurst was to the house, and after dinner I heard him, from another room, mention that a Williamsport man was missing from his family and place of business. Of course I wondered over it, and renewed thoughts of Horace's brutish-looking friend with his mule kept after me as well. But it wouldn't startle me until the following morning when Mrs. Deacon asked me, "Clara, dear, wasn't Horace Wills the name of one of those men who, well, you know," she went softer, "was amongst the others who wronged you, dear, so long ago?"

I was collecting warm ashes, and my hands and my apron were dirty. That dirtiness suddenly mattered to me. "Yes, Elizabeth," I answered her. "He was with them. And he certainly did wrong me."

Then it must have been only two or three weeks later, at a big dinner party hosted by the Deacons that I recall as good fun to cook and serve over, just a regular warm and festive time for all. You see, there was talk and laughter of the Deacons considering getting one of those new water heaters that were coming out, to be put into the big house, perhaps with a big tub and all. I suppose it was the guests picturing Mr. Deacon himself bathing in the tub alongside the contraption that got it all going, before the men settled themselves into discussing the horseless carriage machine that, I at least, guessed other men, perhaps from other countries, were thinking of, or even doing.

But it wouldn't be until the cleaning up that would make that day memorable for me. It was an awful big job for us help, and that's what brought in Mr. Finley, from his duties elsewhere, to move tables and furniture about and all. Anyway, some of the guests were still there, and this one man from Williamsport, who I didn't know the name of, remarked, "What do you men make of that decaying horse found down by the river? The *Gazette* ran the story yesterday."

"Yes, found by boys," remarked Reverend Ashhurst. "Wouldn't be unusual, excepting that the carcass was saddled."

To be brief, the men went on about the story, and of how the constables who investigated found the long-dead horse to belong to the missing hotel and barkeeper, Mr. Horace Wills.

The man I didn't know was earnest. "Well, the mystery deepens due to the horse being obviously slain."

I near shook, and I stole a look to Mr. Finley, who, loaded with two chairs, smiled and nodded to little Sarah Deacon who was momentarily in his way.

I offered cake and ice amongst the men, trying to settle myself as Mr. Deacon furthered the topic with knowledge of his own. "I understand the constables are working on a traveling companion of Mr. Wills, perhaps the last soul to have seen him alive."

And if they told his name I didn't catch it, for all my fears, but I saw his large face I did, at first scary to me, on that frozen road, then stricken with fear amongst those bare trees. Yes, I recalled him all too clear from that cold morning, cloaked in his heavy blankets atop his mule. Then I learned of that certain creatureness about him.

"Yes, but I understand the man's a moron," chimed in the good reverend. "Forever simple-minded. A regular man-child larger than most of the lumbering men."

Then I couldn't hear the things said next due to my own panic, I suppose. But I did steal another look to that Mr. Hank Finley, and it was a good look too. And oh me oh my, I swear it, he never so much as bobbed that big Adam's apple of his, nor batted an eye.

* * *

It wouldn't be until a fortnight or so until I learned the moron's name, through farmhand talk, eavesdropping again. Horace's friend's name was Mr. William Knoebel. He was mostly called "Mr. Billy" I heard, and that he labored for Horace Wills as I had for the fine Deacons.

Somewhere in those weeks, late February or early March, when the winter hangs on in surges, broken up by the promises of the spring to come, I must have started to think differently about having that killer around. As I recall, it began one evening while I was returning from an errand for Mrs. Deacon, down the road to Muncy.

Just two miles or so from home I came across boys, four of them, just youngsters yet, couldn't have been much older than my Emma. Anyway, they were killing a dog. I don't know why. Perhaps one of them got himself bit or something. The point is, I gathered for the most part, after witnessing this, that I never did understand either boys or men. You see, it was such a strange sight how their little gang worked about that nasty business. They grew happy and angry and scared looking, and then back to happy again with their sticks and their rocks. It didn't seem to me, passing upon the wagon, that this clamor was even about the dog, for the poor creature, to my distance, seemed to have lost all its will, wishing only to crawl off somewhere in the weeds to heal or to die. But the boys stayed to her, so cruelly that I wondered later if any one of them could have done it alone, and if it was their togetherness that made them evil like that. Of course it didn't escape me, then upon that road, or later that evening as I saw to my responsibilities, that I somehow felt that the dog could have been me.

I don't know how my watching those boys made me see that Mr. Hank Finley any different, but it just did, with Mr. Finley being alone near every time I saw him. He just didn't seem to be like the other men I knew, those about the farm, the well-off visitors, nor the laboring hands. Oh, I knew for sure that he could harm a soul, save it just seemed to me that it had to be for a powerful, particular reason, for he was always alone, even around others.

Well, March eased on, with its milder, wetter weather. I recall from those early days my watching for Mr. Finley about the farm. When I could see him, he was near always at a distance, and cloaked in his old oilcloth slicker about his duties, with me dry, about my own chores in the big house, watching him through rain-blurred windows. And I can recall serving a certain dinner, inside and to the sounds of a steady hard rain, with the Masons again in attendance, along with newcomers to the farm, Mr. and Mrs. Samuel Wills. Mrs. Deacon whispered to me that morning, "In case you're wondering, Clara, Mr. Wills is related to the missing innkeeper, but distant, very distant."

"I didn't know that," I lied to her, for I really did. "But it's no matter to me, Mrs. Deacon." Which was the truth.

From what I could tell, the men that evening were all in agreement, and had to argue with others not present about the gold standard being superior to a silver standard, and about bank notes, shares and interest rates and other such topics I knew little of.

The gold business, though, must have set me to thinking, for that night I read of it from my Bible, and of men too much concerned over such matters. I found in the Proverbs of Solomon 16:16, "The getting of wisdom is O how much better than gold. And the getting of understanding is to be chosen more than silver." I turned down our oil lamp as low as I could, for Emma was still awake, then I found in the Letter Of James to the Twelve Tribes, James 5:3, "Your gold and silver are rusted away, and their rust will be as a witness against you and will eat your fleshy parts."

Well, those last thoughts scared me, so I snuffed our lamp, and snuggled into our covers, intending to reflect on kinder things. It might seem odd, but Hank Finley came to my thoughts. Then Emma spoke softly, "I had a nice talk with that Mr. Finley, today, out in the bigger part of the house yard."

"You did, honey?" I can still smell her hair. "What did you talk of?"

"I was watching a blue jay, and thought he looked lonely, and Mr. Finley told me that the bird liked it that way. 'It's one of them that winters over,' he told me. 'Stays here by purpose.' "

"Oh my. Anything more?" I asked her.

"Yes, he asked me where I thought that bird lived, and I told him nowhere. Birds don't live anywhere like we do. Then he told me, oh yes they do. If not a nest, then a special tree or some hiding place made soft, and if a body wished they could pick any bird and follow that bird, with patience, to find where that bird lived."

"You talked of birds, did you? So, Mr. Finley likes birds, does he?"

"I guess so," Emma said softly, before telling me more. To be short, I guess he got sporting with her as he was seeing to whatever labor it was that had him in the big yard to begin with. To her delight he also told her that she was free to pick up and name any of the birds she acquainted herself with, "like Rachel the Robin." I believe his words to her were, "due back north, here in this very yard, all proper, in a couple of weeks."

What a queer, funny man. I felt most evil myself for my growing sentiments for him, at least for those sentiments concerning my side of things. You see, by then, I suppose, he had already comforted us both.

* * *

Well, another two or three weeks had come and gone, and it felt near springlike the morning Hank Finley accompanied me to the city, to Williamsport, for the next of my turns of attending to Mrs. Snyder. Mr. Finley would also escort me home in three days hence, for he himself was occupied with several days' worth of transporting dung from the city, so he could save me the Catawissa fare. He used the four-horse team, rigged to the long bed. Its bench seat was broken the year before, and someone replaced it with a smaller one from a child's sleigh. I quietly thought of that, and of wearing a nicer hat, but that might have raised eyebrows, you know.

To be short, the trip provided me my first real talk with Mr. Finley, and he did, indeed, seem gentle and kind, save that secret of mine.

Rounding the Sand Hill Road, near a mile from the farm, I asked him, "Mr. Finley, may I ask you what you did prior to your employment on the farm?"

"Why a little of everything, and not much a'tall, ma'am." He sniffed. "Mostly a boomer for this rail or that." Then he went on, worrying over my confusing his "boomer" work with being a boom-rat for one of the lumbering companies, which I already knew the difference between. Of course I couldn't see him, so much older and all, out on the river hopping amongst all those logs, stamping and branding and doing whatever else those nimble fellows did.

But we did have ourselves a general good talk. I learned of railroading life, and the differences between the "company men" as he called them, with due respect, and the boomers like himself who worked the rails, region to region, living more on trains than proper floors. And I recall his being peacefully mellow over those same men looking down upon their brethren boomers as lowly drifters. He smiled too, and it was the first time I ever saw him do it. He was telling me of their shirts. "Bought new, Miss Waltz, and worn to threads. The company men called 'em 'thousand milers.' "

I asked him of the drinking and fighting I heard so much of about his rough sort of living.

"Oh, ma'am," he replied, watching the road ahead, "there's right dumb fellers everywhere. A body need not sign on with a railroad to find fools."

Well, I knew he was right about that notion. Then I asked him, "Well, how does a boomer go about finding work, and why do they hire you, if they don't take to the drifting sort to begin with?"

He smiled again, looking straight ahead. "We just follow the rails, ma'am, wherever they're hot, as they say. Where there may be the business of a good harvest, or a new factory bein' put up."

Then he paused, reminding the lead gelding to settle down, before going on with, "As for the hiring of us sort, I just keep my dues paid up to whichever railroad brotherhood I take aim to join up with for some work and wages."

Well, we talked on, and he even told me good-naturedly about this joke of "The Indian Valley Line," a made-up railway pike of permanence the boomers were supposedly always looking for. And he told me of the trouble the boomers sometimes had with the "home-guard" as the boomers called the more respectable local men, but most memorable to me now was Mr. Finley's retrieving me three days later, to return me to Montoursville after my stay with Mrs. Snyder.

Making our way through the market square up in Williamsport, we ran into Stacy Kremer, up from his own farm between Muncy and Montgomery. He saw me first.

Miss Waltz!" he called out to me as he strode out toward us, across the wide cobblestone, between two buggies.

Mr. Finley pulled up on the team, as I myself grew suddenly fearful, for I had my secret of course, my sitting beside Horace Wills' very own killer, and still not knowing why he did it.

"Miss Waltz, may I have a moment, please?" he asked me, eyeing Mr. Finley fast, before straightening himself and removing his hat. I noticed that he was balding some. Like myself, eleven years had passed.

"If you would, could I help you down for a moment, just to talk, Miss Waltz? A long time has passed."

I looked to Mr. Finley, who nodded a smile, before helping me down from the wagon. I shouldn't have been so agreeable, but I didn't wish to be rude, and it all came up so fast, you see. But from then on I didn't like it, not from the moment I climbed off. Oh, he was pleasant, overly so, but I found quick that I didn't care anything for his new life, nor for his own farm of, ". . . one hundred and eighty acres, Miss Clara, one hundred and forty put to pasture or plow."

As he talked he looked up often to Mr. Finley, who sat quiet, tending to his own business. In no time then, Mr. Kremer ventured into his first proposal in several years, which made me fear all over again.

"A good, respectable life could be had with me, Miss Clara," he told me, reaching as though to touch me, but I backed up a step. Then I near lost myself when he continued earnestly, and said in a near whisper, "I was the only one who kissed you, and meant it that night, the only one who cared, Miss Clara."

I tried to speak, wanting to tell him that I had to go, but he seemed not to notice, commanding Mr. Finley, "Move your team ahead, man! It's not fitting air for a lady and a gentleman to talk by."

"No disrespect, sir, but I takes my instructions from Mr. Henry Deacon, of Montoursville."

Oh me oh my, how I calmed and suddenly found pride from somewhere.

"If you wish to retain your employment, you'll move your team. I know of Mr. Deacon, through Grange work."

Mr. Finley smiled, and leaned toward us, with his elbows upon his lap. "In Mr. Deacon's absence, such as now, sir, I'll take my instructions from Miss Waltz here."

I turned then to Mr. Kremer, and I tried to whisper, for all the fine folks about. "I'm not interested in any of your ideas. I'm truly not, and I must be off now, for home."

Holding his hat before him, he leaned toward me. "I'll expect nothing from you, Miss Waltz. No dowry or favors. Nothing. Consider your reputation," he whispered.

I spun about and tried to climb the wagon alone. I must have looked a sight with Mr. Finley helping me from one end and with Mr. Kremer helping from the other, with all those good people about. But then that Mr. Kremer came out and said it.

"I hear she favors me, Clara. Your little one, in her appearance."

"Don't you ever mention her. Never again, sir. And don't you ever speak to me again either," hissed out of me, quite by surprise.

"Clara, it could be a new start. So much has changed." He clung to his hat. "Haven't you heard? Even old Horace could be dead, with his horse found kilt down by the river."

"Just stop it." I feared, looking fast to Mr. Finley, then beside me in our seat, who, like himself, remained as calm as anything, about to speak to Mr. Kremer.

But Stacy Kremer spoke first, looking up to me. "His idiot servant stays to the tale, Miss Clara. Says he simply vanished—"

"It's plain, sir," cut in Mr. Finley. "As plain as anything that we have to be moving on now. Good day to ya," he added as his shake of the reins lashed the team into service.

* * *

We rode out of Williamsport in near silence. At first I figured it to be the reference to Horace Wills, or even to his moron servant, Mr. Billy, who Mr. Finley might have, or not have, crossed paths with that dreadful cold morning. But by the time we passed several playing-by-the-roadside kids, I knew or thought different as Mr. Finley brought up the incident himself as, ". . . none of my own affair, Miss Waltz. Nor will any of it become knowledge to anyone about the Deacon house or farm or property, in general."

I put my head down. "I thank you for that, Mr. Finley. I truly do."

"No need, Miss Waltz. As I said before, a body can find right dumb fellers anywhere."

I was learning then that this slender, older-than-me-by-twenty-years man was somebody different from most I'd known. He could be so kind, you see, but save me, what I also learned from within that log that one cold morning.

That night, or at least I believe it was that night, I read from Matthew 5:6, where Jesus was teaching to his disciples: "Happy are those hungering or thirsting for righteousness, since they will be filled." I recall this, you see, because Mr. Kremer was a good man I'm sure, but not good enough, for he was there that night, and he did help himself to me, and then help the others help themselves. So, I suppose I had been hungering too, for something ever since, just as I didn't understand what Stacy Kremer wanted or needed of me. And, of course, as for Mr. Finley, I had no idea at all what made him thirst to do what I saw him do.

* * *

No company came for a spell to the big farmhouse. As usual, this began to work on the Deacons, for Mr. Deacon would turn to Mrs. Deacon for his concerns. And she, in turn, would honestly try to care for his conversations. Through this spell, I recall one of his concerns being our president of then, Benjamin Harrison, and how, according to Mr. Deacon, the congress was seizing the reins anyway, and then more, of which I knew none of, about election votes mattering over regular ones. "The man has no right to his office to begin with!" proclaimed Mr. Deacon. Poor Mrs. Deacon, she listened on to his cares, and to others about the throwing open of Oklahoma to settlers the year before, and to the army finally settling things with the savages just months before at a place called Wounded Knee. He was right about this last thing, and Mrs. Deacon agreed, and meant it. "The brutish things are such a problem, Henry. I guess a problem we're all weary of," I recall her answering him.

As for myself in those weeks, I came to gather that Mr. Finley, who I queerly feared, yet prayed over, must have never told a soul of my meeting up with Stacy Kremer, for I heard nothing of it, not from the help, nor from Mrs. Deacon. And in that time I also began to run into him, Mr. Finley that is, more and more about the farm. I think he was meaning it to happen, or perhaps the both of us were, in a quiet, careful way.

The first of our quiet times together, or the second, if one wishes to figure the two wagon rides, came shortly after the Deacons bought two shiny new safety bicycles. This new type, with both wheels the same size, and all over the place nowadays, were all the talk back then. It being mid-March, Mr. and Mrs. Deacon probably purchased the new bicycles in preparation for their leisure of the new spring, which was warming to us day by day. Anyway, this freed up the two old high-wheelers for the bigger children, and for one Sunday evening, for Mr. Finley and myself, of course after being properly invited and all.

Mr. Finley was about the house, you see, reporting to Mr. Deacon, then tidying up about the big yard when he happened upon the high-wheelers, and then myself.

"Miss Waltz, is your work done, and if so would you care for a bicycle ride?" he asked me from beneath that big brimmed hat.

Well, I replied of course that I'd have to check inside first, where I consulted Mrs. Deacon, who smiled her approval, which shied me up. To be short, within the hour we were riding the high-wheelers up into town on Broad Road, and then up the bumpy cobblestones of Loyalsock Avenue, past our church, which gave me something to talk about.

"No, ma'am. I can't rightly say that I do subscribe to the Good Book about most things," he told me, not shy himself. "As a boy I got some of the teachings, but I never took to the meetins', then nor now, to be truthful."

"I go," I told him. "Every Sabbath." I nearly toppled my high-wheeler from a rut I come upon. But naturally I didn't tell him since when I'd been going so regular.

Then, with one of Mr. Deacon's concerns in mind, I brought up the Indians out west, asking him, "Did you ever see any, besides those in the circus shows?"

"Yes, ma'am, I have, but years and years ago, out along the Mississippi," he said as he watched the road ahead. "I surely don't care to fall from this thing before ya and all. I'd look like a right dumb feller, wouldn't I?" He smiled down at his high-wheeler from behind his bony cheekbones.

"Tell me about the savages," I asked him, hoping to come upon a subject we could pass the time on.

"Oh, Miss Clara, them ones wasn't much to tell of. I was all excited as a boy I'd bet, but there was nothing wild about them times. The Indians I saw was about the same as them you see in the traveling shows, 'cepting they themselves had no show to join up with, I guess."

"There must have been some nasty fighting going on with them though," I added, just to talk as I peddled along.

"Sure, farther west," he said rather quietly. "But that ain't what got them fool-hearted people. It was liquor, cholera, small pox and more liquor. A month's trappin' bartered off for a single night's drinkin'. They made no sense. Dirty brutes at times, I understand, yet one and all as simple as children."

Well I pondered that point, I did, and by then we were outside of the collection of houses that was Montoursville back then, so we turned and headed back, away from the eastern farms, down smoother Montour Street, with both of us perhaps not wanting to tire out our little time together.

And as we peddled along, I was suddenly wondering deep of Mr. Finley, and so quick and odd-like that I startled when he spoke to me as we were well into town.

"I wish to thank ya, Miss Clara, for this bicycle riding time. It's been quite a while for me."

"Riding high-wheelers?" I asked.

"Well, that too." He smiled. "But I was meanin' good, quiet company. So I'll thank you for both, ma'am," he said as he nodded to me briefly.

"You're welcome, Mr. Finley," my voice broke, as I watched for the cobblestones to turn to brick ahead of us.

Then shortly we were back at the Deacon farm, where Mr. Finley took the high-wheelers away. I probably thought of him, that night I'm sure, because I did think about him in those spring days to follow, as the mystery of the missing Horace Wills was even brought up in Sunday services by Reverend Ashhurst. It seemed I couldn't rid myself of the bad side of this new acquaintance of mine. Lord, how I feared and shamed, sitting there with Emma, listening to the Good Message, feeling so alone, save myself, with my evil knowledge of that business.

So, all alone, I read about it, just as I had to live my days with it. I read of a confession from the letter of James to the Twelve Tribes that were scattered about. I thought so over 5:16, "Therefore openly confess your sins to one another and pray for one another, that you may be healed. A righteous man's supplication, when it is at work, has much force." I wondered first, after setting my Bible beside my sleeping Emma, if either he or I was righteous enough to help one another. Then my lonely ponderings led me to forgiveness, and to Jesus' sending forth His disciples in John 20:23, "If you forgive the sin of any persons, they stand forgiven to them; if you retain those of any persons, they stand retained." I thought about this too, and wondered, and half hoped that perhaps we were the only ones able to help one another, or, and I feared over it, to damn one another.

* * *

Then came awful days. Before this, of course, I wondered over just what Mr. Finley might have known or heard concerning Emma and myself. I was quite certain that the farm help talked, but I had no idea how much nor how often, but perhaps it's little matter. You see, little Emma herself came to overhear such talk of myself.

"Mama," she told me one night, "I heard some of the men talking, in the lower barn, and I think they meant you."

"What did they say?" I asked her.

And then she told me, and oh me oh my, it was talk such as I hadn't heard in a long time. I guessed it was stirred up from all the Horace Wills speculation that was going around about then. It was that awful thinking of some men concerning women of circumstances such as my own, figuring we somehow asked for what had happened to us, and then more speculation about most women secretly desiring that evilness. Only, before my little Emma, they were talking such painful idleness about me.

"Did they talk such stuff before you, Emma?"

"No, Mama. I was on the other side of the long corncrib. They didn't know I was there. And I tiptoed out."

Well that much was good, and of course I could, and did set her right, and I soothed her too, but then I thought of Mr. Finley, and a sad faith came over me. About his responsibilities he too had room enough about his duties and labors about the big farm to be amongst such conversations.

I was more sad than angry. I knew Mr. Finley was a killer, so it made no sense, but I still didn't want him thinking such stuff about myself.

Late one evening about those days I stumbled upon my own sentiments in Paul to the Galatians, from Galatians, 6:4 and 6:5, "But let each one prove what his own work is, and then he will have cause for exaltation in regard for himself alone, and not in comparison with the other person. For each one will carry his own load." This wisdom turned my thoughts to Mr. Finley, for he surely must have carried a burden of his own, just as I carried mine.

* * *

Near to the end of March, to Mr. Deacon's great relief for fitting company, there came a big dinner party that I don't believe will ever fade from my mind, for so much turned about that evening in those early days of these events. It was most fine weather you see, and the company came early, as invited. The big east lawn was cut for the croquet that would surely please the ladies and the gentlemen guests. The lawn looked fine, all evened out, like a near summer lawn to me.

And I remember it being a quite sporting game that day. I forget who won, perhaps one of Mr. Deacon's friends from Williamsport who I didn't know much of. The Reverend Ashhurst created much gaiety, though, with his earnest play, once driving one woman's second ball off the cut part of the lawn entirely. I observed this, naturally, while serving the teas, beverages and cakes to all who partook. I also quietly fancied, that afternoon and across the days to come, my own self dressed just as finely as I stroked my own two balls about. They were both blue ones to be silly and day-dreamy enough, and to be truthful, and perhaps wrong, I rounded the wickets in my fancy with none else save that Mr. Finley.

I was happy the day of that party, I suppose having moved on from worrying over the talk of the farmhands. Even tending to that big spread of a dinner was pleasant and fun. Little Emma worked right alongside me, acting all grown up. Of course the men, they talked on regarding their own concerns, along with their separate opinions over this and that. A Williamsport banker went on about the failed efforts of steamboat travel upon our Susquehanna River: "Given up nearly eighty years ago. She's a shallow one, without a constant deep channel." Which I gather led the men to grand views of these steam-powered tractors out west.

"They call the farms out there bonanzas," our own Mr. Deacon exclaimed.

"Tons and tons of wheat," returned a heavily bearded man whom I didn't know. "Why it's nothing short of rivers of food, I tell you, my good friends. Mountains of grain grown and gathered from the plains, then sold in Chicago, St. Louis and Kansas City, then railroaded east."

But the women come back to me best from that day, for all their pretty outfits and dresses. Most wore sporting dresses, for the lawn games and such. And of course those new safety bicycles were gotten out and ridden about, as some of the others graced the afternoon finely in that style of their dresses that reminded one of upholstery or drapery, all sewn about with fringe and tassel. Those were the ladies who stayed inside about the phonograph that spun continuously after dessert, or out upon the veranda, chatting of fashion, children and any other newsy thing.

You see, I suppose I began once again to concern myself over such cares as appearances that spring. The look, of course, was full-hipped and full bosomed, and I was neither. It was called the hourglass look. Prior to that spring I took my guide on such matters from the First Letter to Timothy, from 2:9 and 2:10, "Likewise I desire the woman to adorn themselves in well arranged dress, with modesty and soundness of mind, not with styles of hair braiding and gold or pearls or very expensive garb, but in the way that befits women professing to reverence God, namely through good works." I tried, you see, to stay true to Paul's notion on the matter, for in times when I felt most all alone and unloved, I was most soothed by Acts 3:19, "Repent, therefore, and turn around so as to get your sins blotted out, that seasons of refreshing may come from the person of Jehovah." And oh me oh my, how I longed for a season such as that.

Well, that splendid afternoon did wear on, and since most stuffed themselves good from our earlier big spread, we tended to the guests with cakes and pies and such as they tired about the big house and yard. I do recall one earnest conversation about big bones of stone, of horrid big creatures, said to be long since gone, being dug up out west to be railroaded back east. "Dinosaurs is the favored name," guided Mr. Deacon himself in the talk.

"We must be careful," warned the Williamsport banker. "We all remember the 'Cardiff Giant,' don't we? Up in New York State? Circus acts are everywhere it seems. Maybe lost from their own traveling shows!" This brought laughter.

"The world's not that old," warned the good reverend with a smile. "And bones are bone, and stone comes from stone. We're always wise to be cautious with our newer enthusiasms."

I recall this for I myself was most skeptical, as were a good many other Christians, for Genesis never mentioned such beasts. I also recall this business for it was Mr. Finley himself, who was not even a church-going man, who advised me tenderly on the subject later that spring, for he himself was smitten with those ideas. "The way a body might see it, Clara, is that them Bible words was writ a long time ago, and maybe that knowledge weren't seen as fit to tell at the time is all. At least not for them people that they was writ for, ya see."

But I'm off my tracks here. What tied that day's events of fine things, hardy food and good conversation to my memory was the arrival of Mr. Watson's eldest boy, Joshua, up from the farms along the river. He galloped in happy, with horrid news for the men smoking upon the veranda.

"A body's washed up!" he sung out. "Downriver, just upstream from the Muncy Railroad Depot."

The good Reverend Ashhurst spoke first, reminding the men, "We're in the company of ladies and children. Let us keep our voices down."

Working the veranda, I myself was startled. The banker chewed hard at his flaring cigar. "They know who it is, the corpse?"

"If they do, they're not sayin'," answered young Mr. Watson.

Then I retreated into the kitchen of the big house, finding a reason to do so, for my hands began to shake. I can still recall Mr. Deacon commenting that the Muncy Railroad station sat oddly on the opposite side of the river from the town itself. "Impractical for commerce," were his words. For the rest of the story I'd have to wait and bide my concerned time, listening about the big house and farm for any more dead man talk.

* * *

It must have taken three days at the most, and worrisome ones too, as I took to daydreaming about Mr. Finley's possible past as I tended to my daily responsibilities. I wondered over where else he might have been, and what else he might have done. Of course I also saw him about the property, but he never seemed to be any different with all the dead man talk about. And I think this made me ponder him deep then, making me feel I had to back up from him, so to speak, in terms of what little we did have to do with one another.

Indeed, I even wondered if the dead man found was even the remains of Horace Wills. It could have been the carcass of someone else. It could have been the remains of anyone. And I recall the weather growing fickle, and cold again for a spell as March grew to a close. And I also recall remembering a soap sculpture that as a foolish girl of fifteen or so, I fashioned out of a big cake of lye. It wound up as two doves, breast to breast, lovebirds I suppose. You see, I fancied back then that I could work up the forwardness to give them to Joseph Logan as a token of my feelings.

And then those thoughts led me off to the probable Joseph Logan of that spring, married and all, up in Newberry in a decent home with a decent life, probably in touch from time to far time with his brother, still with the circus, another of my distant attackers of so long ago now.

And then, of course, the news came to me, as Emma and I busied ourselves over the Deacons' washing. Mrs. Deacon herself, kind Elizabeth, toting her baby Ellen, must have felt the duty was her own.

"Emma, dear," she started out, "can you excuse your mother and I? Just for a few minutes. We need to be alone here on the back porch."

Emma scampered off with a nod from myself.

"Please sit down, Clara," Elizabeth said as she sat in the only other chair.

Then promptly, and softly, she told me, "The body of the dead man they found down Muncy way is none other than that of Mr. Horace Wills."

"Thank you for telling me, and thank you for thinking of me," I answered her, smoothing out my apron.

"Well, I do so, Clara, because of what you quietly and boldly shared with Mr. Deacon and myself back when we first interviewed you."

I thanked her again, but in a swirl of thought, as I pondered that defiler of myself, that man who did seem so to lead the events of that awful night of the swinging lantern. And with my head down I recalled the laughter of the men, and then my clothes being torn from me in my struggle.

Mrs. Deacon then reached to me and touched me, awakening me almost, and I nodded and forced a smile. She asked me if I was all right, and I told her that I was, thanking her again. Then she rose and left me to my responsibilities, as I thought about hate after that news, of how it's so wrong, so un-Christian, and so hard to push back down into yourself, where a stronger person can hide it and live with it. I thought of how easily quenched it can be, and of all the evil in that. Then I thought of

Mr. Finley, and wondered over what on earth did he hate so to do what he did. I also knew of his whereabouts that afternoon. He was set to work with a team, hauling thirteen hundred bushels of lime up from the Montoursville Depot. I wondered if he was simply roaming now, perhaps searching for something. It couldn't have been my own revenge, but he happened upon a piece of it. And it was this last notion that I hated to be true to myself about.

Then that very evening it came to me, and to all of us, all official, printed up in the *Williamsport Gazette*. The bold front-page story called him ". . . an innkeeper, a local businessman and a family man."

"The officials determined that he wasn't robbed," Mr. Deacon added, "due to his having over fifty-two dollars in his pocket-book, still in his trousers." He and Elizabeth had joined me in the kitchen with their coffee as I tidied up my after-supper work.

"Which is how they identified him," cut in Mrs. Deacon.

"Yes it is, dear," conceded Mr. Deacon. "And being that his horse turned up slain some time back they're eyeing it as a murder."

That word alone sent a chill through me.

The story, which of course became all the talk, also stated that his body, dead possibly over two months by then, was found jammed between logs cut and branded by the K & M Schoch Company.

"What the *Gazette* didn't print," Mr. Deacon then went quieter, "for the decency of his family about, is that he was found faceless. Eaten away at near clean from the bones."

Elizabeth and I stilled ourselves.

"The snapping turtles of the early spring," Mr. Deacon figured aloud.

CHAPTER 5

Just two days had passed since the body of Horace Wills turned up, and then came new news, which had all up in a clamor all over again. Oh me oh my, how I can recall this part all so clear.

Another man killed. Up in Newberry. Murdered in the night upon his own brother's porch was how we first heard the talk of it.

I myself came to hear of this horrid business the afternoon that Rebecca Snyder came to stay the day. You see, her husband, Mrs. Snyder's youngest boy, was looking into buying a leather tannery over on Washington Street, and asked Mr. Deacon to accompany him to that place of trade. I suppose both killings seemed all so sudden, back to back it would have seemed to all else, with the discovery of Mr. Wills' body only two days before. Of course, to me, two months and beyond had passed since Horace Wills was killed. No, I didn't feel the same despair and shock, nor would I for another two days to come.

As I tended to Mr. Snyder's and Rebecca's visiting, I can still recall Rebecca's banter about "oh, this baby's this . . ." and "this baby's that . . ." You see, they were married the spring before and she was, by this visiting, well along with carrying her first-born, and greatly enjoyed talking of her condition. She did so as she had regarding her wedding well before it had taken place, as though she had been through both events a number of times before. But now, at putting this to paper, I suppose in her own way she had, as other women probably have too, in their young-girl hearts as children and beyond as they dreamed of such big days while paying mind to those like days of others. My own such ponderings, I suppose, melted away long ago. In any event, I'm off my story, I see.

Young Mr. Snyder returned with Mr. Deacon, and both came into the big house looking serious, stricken with more than any unpromising news concerning the business they attended to.

"Oh my, look at you two. What could have both of you looking so full of gloom?" Rebecca chimed as they handed their wraps to me, just inside the big front door.

Mr. Deacon looked to Mrs. Deacon, then to me, before looking back to his wife. He started to say something, but Mr. Snyder cut him off.

"Perhaps not here, Henry," he said as he nodded, I was certain, toward me.

"Don't be silly, James." Mr. Deacon was fast. "Clara can hear this. Good Lord, everyone's going to learn of the matter shortly. Indeed, up and down the valley and beyond."

"What is it?" Elizabeth asked him as she went to her husband's side, accompanying him into the parlor.

"Another killing. A murder for sure, Elizabeth."

"Oh my," gasped Rebecca Snyder. "James, tell us all about it. Who told you, and who, pray, is it this time?"

I hung their coats and hats, and went for tea and more cakes, listening to those in the parlor behind me as best I could. I caught only pieces of course, being first about my duties in the kitchen. But it didn't come to me as frightful hearsay as it must have to them, but more as deep pains, more of my life about that early spring, being dark and evil, breaking apart or coming together, powerful and out of all-seeming control. I heard Mr. Deacon's ". . . a man's dead. Up in Newberry, overnight."

And James Snyder's ". . . maybe late at night . . ." as I came out with their cakes and tea.

Mr. Deacon followed with, "The murdered man was found face down." And I quivered so, rattling the tea cups and cream bowl upon the tray as James Snyder told the room in general, "Harold Elmer told us not to say anything, but an ax was driven clean down through the man, fastening him into the planks of the porch. Right down through the dead man's back, through his cape, straight-coat and all."

"Good Lord in Heaven," murmured Rebecca. "A beast of a killer."

"Harold's just a deputy constable," Mr. Deacon reminded all in his calmer voice. "And quite new to it. Perhaps he's a bit taken by it all. And let us keep in mind that he got his story at least third or fourth hand. Things can change with each telling, especially specifics and details," he added, straightening himself in his big chair, dusting nothing from his vest that I could see.

"Sounded detailed enough for me," answered the much younger James Snyder. "Particulars such as an ax driven entirely through a man's body, wedging him fast to the lumber of a porch, sounds too awful a subject to be twisted about much." Then he wrung his hands together. "You heard him, Henry, tell of the one Williamsport constable. Enforcing the law for fifteen years and yet got sick at the site of the crime." Then he paused. "Them working that bloody ax loose from the planking, up through the ribs and spine of a fellow man, as another constable wept, he on the force five years or more."

My own mind whirled again, to the safety of my Emma, at school, busy at her learning, safe with the other youngsters at the wooden schoolhouse out Loyalsock Avenue that midday. Then of course to that Mr. Hank Finley, that thin, quiet man that I had ridden the high-wheelers with not but a week before, passing Emma's very same schoolhouse. I only ever witnessed but one killing of a man in all my life, so naturally I figured it to be him. So did everyone else, I was sure, whoever he might have been, save without what I had, the secret of his face and his name, without my own wonderings of why on earth was he doing it.

* * *

The next few days hummed and feared with the news, both hushed and aloud. Most, of course, was speculation and notions of proper retribution for the killer, and naturally, wonderings and stories over just who the second man killed even was, for the officials about the case up in the city were keeping quiet at first, for some official reason or another. For me, though, they were days like ones already lived, and I was tired of them as such.

Again I toiled about my duties and responsibilities, fretting most senselessly for the safety of Emma. About the big house, I also wondered why I was so calm at times, and unable to cry when I wished so that I could, especially late at night. I wondered those nights, tucked in with my sleeping Emma, if I was committing yet another crime by not turning that Mr. Finley in to the law for the first one, and oh me oh my, would such justice have prevented the second killing from coming to be?

They were days that brought back memories of my own most terrible night, memories such as I hadn't had for near two months then, and years and years prior to then. I felt dirty, and bathed full and proper three days before the week's end, trying my hardest to keep them quiet, away from my life about the big house. One of them was of one of my attackers calling me ". . . a poor substitute for a real woman . . ." and ". . . a little whore . . ." really wanting their wrath. It still hurts as I reflect, but just a touch, and only for the young girl that I was back then.

But back to those days just after the second killing. They were indeed hard ones to get through. In seeing after Emma, I thought of her lost sister, little Ellie. You see, I used to fancy at times that her spirit was all of eleven years, just as Emma's, save forever wiser than all of us. And I took to imagining her as somehow watching over us, unable to help us, but watching us and loving us nonetheless—watching all of us as an angel, her sister with whom she shared my womb, myself, her mournful mother, and maybe even that Mr. Hank Finley, whoever he was, who I avoided as quietly and as busily as I could manage at the time.

Of course there was much talk of the mysterious second victim, and even more to do with his killer still at large. The victim hearsay ran two ways, one a mere teen, the other a crippled older fellow who pleaded in vain for his miserable life. The killer talk, however, settled easier, drawing itself up into a crazed logger, for it had to be a strong man, you see. The whisperings and nodding each came from one reliable source or another, from some cousin, or from some friend of some deputy constable, or even from the Newberry family itself, said, in hushed tones, to be taken into hiding up Spook Hollow, west of the city, just as so many of those escaping coloreds were forty years before. This strongest talk favored a logger fresh down from New York State. Some had him marred with logger's small pox, which was any pattern of scars gotten from a fight with another logger while the other happened to be wearing his tree-climbing irons. They were rough men, you see. But then the talk straightened a bit with the timely news being at last permitted to run in the *Gazette*, and oh me oh my, how I did fear once more, all alone, save myself and my little Emma.

The story was, of course, a big front-pager, and the attention of everyone east and west up that Susquehanna Valley. The victim, near cut into halves, but not printed up as such, was none other than ". . . Mr. Charles Franklin Logan, 34 years of age, formerly of Cogan Station . . ."

Another of my attackers, and this having come to me not but three weeks after I pondered on so regarding how nice his brother Joseph's home probably was up there in Newberry, with a life so unlike my own back then, with him having proper employment, a good wife and with young ones and all. But back to Charles Logan, murdered Charlie, dead at thirty-four. Lord save me, but I couldn't help myself from figuring in my head how this event put him at twenty-two or so back when he helped himself to me, you see.

I waited until I could be alone to read more thorough from Mr. Deacon's *Gazette*, so it took me another day of waiting. But I waited, for I already felt as though others about our small town were somehow watching me whenever I had to go up into Broad Street for anything. And I felt this about the farm and the big house too, for as with my other attackers, I also made no secret of Charlie Logan being amongst those men that night.

And I wondered if a tale like mine could cling to an area for a dozen years, especially if reawakened. So my reading of Mr. Deacon's *Gazette* was a slow and a thorough one. And I tried to picture Charlie as I read, him with a dozen years added to his life. The story told of his still being with the Big Show Circus, which wintered over in the Deep South. At that time the show was still far off, down in the city of Philadelphia, where Charlie "took leave" to visit friends and family in and about Williamsport, to pick back up with his employment, meeting the circus, over in Scranton, in coal country. The story also stated that the very same show was scheduled to play out up in Williamsport that June to come, the very circus Charlie took Joe off to all those years before. It then gave a brief description of Charlie, a most kind one, probably provided by the same family and friends, before closing with nothing of his killer, purposely stating, ". . . the *Gazette* will not be a party in hampering the investigation intent upon bringing this beast amongst us to a fitting justice."

That night, with Emma still awake, eyeing the ceiling, I read from the song of Moses, in Deuteronomy, for I believed that the newest of my few friends must have surely committed both killings. I must have read verses 32:32–35 three or four times through: "For their vine is from the vine of Sodom and from the terraces of Gomorrah. Their grapes are grapes of poison, their clusters are bitter. Their wine is the venom of serpents and the cruel poison of cobras." And then: "Vengeance is mine. At the appointed time their feet will move unsteadily, for the day of their disaster is near." And I gathered myself with that, tucking Emma into our bedding, wondering if those words were reserved for the deeds of my attackers, or for those of that Mr. Finley, or for the likes of them both.

Oh, how I didn't know my own self back then, for I wanted to hate that Mr. Finley, for whatever he was an agent of. Then, and it was after Emma had fallen off to sleep, fresh memories stole their way loose within me, memories of how it hurt so in that shed that night. Not overall, you see, but of how particular that one pain was, and over and over again. Oh how I wanted to cry, but couldn't as I hugged at Emma. Perhaps my little angel, Ellie, was doing it for me, for I just couldn't do it, for it was Charlie Logan who was the first one to strike me that awful night. He struck me when I began fighting back. And my one fresh memory was that his striking me was the lesser pain, the one high up, in the middle of my face.

* * *

I should have known what the quick glances and the quiet whisperings about town would come to, but just the same I was taken aback when they led to myself being questioned that first time. Again I was hard after the washing upon the back porch. And I recall it was trying to be sunny out that morning, for naturally I watched the skies on washing days. It also had to be a Monday or a Thursday, also due to the washing, you see. But I do recall it was the first of April, the Fool's Day, some couple of days after I read all I could from Mr. Deacon's *Gazette*.

There was a hushed movement to the front of the big house as I worked, but the Deacons' farm was big and busy so that wasn't anything uncommon, not until Mr. Deacon himself, dressed quite well, as for business, came out back for me, all solemn, asking me to, "Tidy up now, Clara. And be quick about it. We have official guests who wish to speak with you." Then he must have seen something in my face, for he followed it with, "Constables, Clara. Two from the city, with Amos as well, so you'll have one of our own."

I put down my work, realizing the shake in my hands, trying awful to rid myself of it as I hurried up to my room, to brush out my hair and tie on a fresh apron. Upon collecting myself, I returned to the parlor to find myself amongst Mr. and Mrs. Deacon sitting beside Montoursville's own high constable, Mr. Amos Reese, who was the biggest man in the room, and two other men, deputy constables from Williamsport, one of whom who introduced himself as Constable Ralph Keeler, in charge of the Charles Logan murder. As I entered, they were debating where best to seat me. For some reason I asked all in the room, "Is there anything I may serve you, gentlemen?"

"Clara, dear," Elizabeth Deacon nearly whispered, "please be seated," as she ushered me to the wooden chair in the corner,

Sarah's chair, as though I was her eldest daughter. But it was a warm thing to do.

"If Miss Waltz isn't a suspect, Constable Keeler," Henry Deacon said as he straightened himself, "then my own parlor should serve you well. Your privacy can be assured."

Our own high constable, barrel-chested Amos Reese, spoke quietly, "Constable, if I may, the Deacons are of the finest of people about our town, and they've allowed their own home to become home to Miss Waltz here, and her daughter too for that matter, for, well, for some time now. I move that we proceed."

The other deputy only nodded, staying silent, standing so straight beside Constable Keeler that he looked to be almost leaning backwards.

"Elizabeth, will you excuse us? And no refreshments, please," Henry Deacon spoke to his wife.

Mrs. Deacon, in her big blue dress, then swept quietly from the parlor, closing the double doors behind her without so much as a glance toward me and my predicament. And oh me oh my, I could have used one.

"Perhaps a couple more chairs, Mr. Deacon?" the silent deputy asked, which would be his only words throughout. And then, in short order, the three constables seated themselves, cornering me as Henry Deacon stood behind them, beginning a silent, slow pacing, mostly looking at the floor.

"As I stated," began that Mr. Keeler, in a deeper voice, "we're gathered here, Miss Waltz, to ask you of any knowledge you may have concerning the murder of Mr. Charles Logan."

I breathed a good deal easier. "I know nothing. Only what I read in Mr. Deacon's *Gazette*." You see, this was a subject on which I had only pondered, and truly knew nothing of. I could cling to the truth here.

"Now, Miss Waltz," he said as he leaned forward on his dinner chair from the big table, "stories long since about have it that you once claimed that Mr. Logan, one time, long ago, well, took his own cruel way with you, in a manner of putting it."

"They'd be true, sir, if stories such as that are about."

"Was he alone in this, this most evil crime, ma'am?"

"No, sir. There were four others."

"When did this happen?"

I breathed deep. "Nearly twelve years ago, sir."

"Why didn't you come forward then? Surely there was law and order up Cogan Station way," he said, as he let on, whether he cared to or not, that he already had at least some of the story.

"I did, sir," I answered, looking about, trying to answer them all. "But no one did anything for me. Not even my father." At this, Mr. Deacon stilled himself to look sadly to me.

"It comes mighty curious, Miss Waltz, to not only me, but to a growing handful of authorities, that now two men are dead, both killed at the hands of another," he stressed, "with both of 'em so accused by yourself of such a monstrous offense." Then he paused. "A third man's lucky to have gotten himself lost in riverside woods, or he might'a died for being a witness. Do you by any chance know the simpleton once employed by Mr. Horace Wills?"

"No, I don't. My life is in service to the Deacons."

"I didn't think so," he said as he breathed deeply.

The mentioning of Horace Wills and his servant, "Mr. Billy", did start me though. I didn't care to do any lying, you see. But I angered too, for my recent memories coming to me as they had.

"I didn't accuse anyone of anything," I spoke up. "I told on them men is all. There's a difference." I spoke more to the Williamsport constables. "At least to me who went through it, and all it brought onto me."

"You're certain, are you, of the accurate identity of these five fellows?"

"Of course I am," I replied and lowered my face and wished I hadn't.

Big Amos Reese readjusted his large self in his own dinner chair and asked the Williamsport constables, "Is this the train of questioning you men figure is best?"

"Just a little farther, sir," that Mr. Keeler replied, never looking at Amos. "Could you recall, ma'am, in all due respect, the order of exactly how these men did what you claim they did? Or, more simply, who was the first, the second and so on as you claim this crime to have happened?"

I thought a spell, but just a short one. Then I saw Mr. Deacon turn away to this one, as though studying his own parlor walls. "I can, sir, for most all of it, but not toward the end of it, however long or brief it was. For it was my life's darkest hour, and I don't care to spell it out for a room full of near strangers. It belongs to prayer. I truly believe that, sir."

"Then tell me this." He settled himself a bit, for I thought he got a touch sore as he began wringing his hands. "Are you at all pleased now? You know, learning of the eventual fates of two of these fellow men?"

"No, I am not. I wish I could recite for you from Paul to the Romans, but I won't get it right." The men stayed silent. Then I went on with, "You could seek it out for yourselves if you care to."

"We're listening, Miss Waltz," kind Amos prodded me. Constable Keeler gave him a fast look.

"We're not to return evil for evil to anyone is what I know. We're to be peaceable toward one another. And vengeance is not ours, but His." My voice shook a bit.

"It's just god-awful odd, ma'am." Mr. Keeler was quick. "A coincidence of near unimaginable odds! Two men linked together only by you as far as anyone knows, and now both dead. And of course, a third, a moron who could have seen something."

"They were both in the circus together, I understood back then," I offered quietly to all the men before me.

"But the circus is far off, down in the city of Philadelphia!" He raised his voice. Then he quieted and nearly smiled as he added, "And you're here, Miss Waltz, a mere train ride up the Catawissa from the one pried loose from the planks of his brother's porch, and not but a couple of fishing holes from the remains of the slain horse of the other."

Mr. Deacon spun fast, as though to reclaim his own parlor. "I thought all were in accord that it had to be a man, a big strong man."

"Oh, I do believe that. I do believe that to be true," replied Constable Keeler, looking only to me in my corner in my clean apron. "But he done it for a reason. A killer and his reason. Find one, either one, and you get yourself led to the other."

Big Amos Reese then grew with his own standing. "Clara's practically a shadow about these parts," he said, directing his thoughts toward the Williamsport deputy constables. "I can understand your earnestness. I hope we never have a killing around here ourselves . . ."

"You already have," came smugly from that Mr. Keeler, which may have insulted Amos Reese, for he went stern.

"What I'm saying is, it could be a coincidence, and probably is if Clara here is your best of leads. The new immigration we've been seeing about, they mostly speak English, and some right well, but we don't truly know who or what them people are. Why, I understand the steamship companies purposely exagger-ate American opportunities just to sell their own tickets. And the railroads too, sending recruiters abroad, all over Europe, eager to fill out federal grant lands, with neither of these enterprises caring what becomes of these people, nor our own."

Then he pardoned himself to all, and sat back down, closing with, "Clara here, church-going Miss Clara Waltz, the mother of a little one as quiet as herself—she just can't be your only lead."

Oh, I felt powerful evil just then, with that big, kind Amos Reese praising me so, shielding me from those city deputies when I did indeed know of at least Hank Finley's part in some of it. So I lowered my face and hid in my corner as the men talked on, but not for long, and I can't recall what all they went on about, but shortly the Williamsport deputy constables were gone. On their way home, I figured.

* * *

The following days passed gray, in a lasting, cold rain that seemed to weep steady and slow for me as I prayed, and swung from hating that Mr. Hank Finley to hating myself, and then to hating the both of us. And I cried some too, hopelessly for myself, and hiding it, as I was about my responsibilities in the pantry and about the rooms above the big house, always within listening, it seemed, to that wet sky all over outside.

I wish I could recall more from those days that followed that first time I was questioned, but it's probably more proper that I can't. I did stumble upon, then reflect upon Proverbs 27:2, which went: "May a stranger, and not your own mouth praise you; may a foreigner, and not your own lips do so." Well, both Mr. Deacon and our own high constable, Amos Reese, did praise me, but you see, they weren't my stranger, for that Mr. Finley from the south most surely was, and I was burdened with what I did see him do.

So I prayed through those days, wanting and wishing the Lord to understand my lostness, my lonesomeness and my fear, and I pained so over not being able to properly sort out any of them to offer to my Savior.

CHAPTER 6

Another week passed. The gray skies from the west had moved on, leaving the fields wet and muddy, and the early mornings and the late nights damp and chilly, as the clear skies warmed the lengthening days with a crisp spring air at last.

From those warming days, I can recall one particular visiting dinner party as clearly as I can recall the budding of the bushes and the trees, and the spring grass suddenly all evenly green but not evenly tall. Although a pleasant visit and conversation for the Deacons and their guests, that early evening would weigh heavy upon myself and my ponderings.

In attendance that early afternoon, and on into the early evening were of course the Deacons and their fine children, the Reverend Ashhurst and Mr. and Mrs. Mason. Also dining with the Deacons were James and Rebecca Snyder, with Rebecca of course claiming to be just too large with child, most certainly carrying twins.

Supervised by Mrs. Deacon, Emma and myself ate earlier as we prepared that fine big spread about a nice ham. Mrs. Deacon of course joined her guests upon their arrival to properly see to their entertainment, leaving Emma and I to the work of seeing everyone fed full and proper, which the both of us enjoyed doing together. In our bed, for three nights before, Emma even began suggesting alterations for the laying of the linen and the silver and dishes, which were under her growing charge.

Across that big meal was talk of news, both local and broad, and a good deal of business, which took the table several times to James Snyder's acquiring of that Washington Street tannery. It must have been in the process of trading hands, but as I stated before, I knew nothing of such matters, save for the awful smell of tannery work. But then, toward the end of the main dining, after the children were excused to tables set up in the sitting room for their desserts, the talk of the adults turned to the recent news of the murdering of Charles Logan. James Snyder brought it up as I was off in the kitchen. Then I heard Mr. Mason answer him, then James again.

"It's most sad that he was at home in a way," claimed James, as I entered the parlor with a fine pie. "I'd figure probably on a furlough of sorts from his circus employment, not unlike the army."

But most eyes about the big table batted cat-like to myself. And then all quieted uneasily as I placed the warm pie and went to work gathering up the remaining dinner plates and soiled silver.

Mr. Deacon rose slow and deliberate, spreading both his hands, claiming the corners of his own big dinner table. Slowly he proclaimed, "I won't tolerate this quietness about this subject in the company of our own dear Clara. Such behavior falls too close to suspicion, implicating a person so gentle in her conduct. A woman as near a part of my very own family as a person in my employ could be."

All remained quiet, save for mother-to-be, Rebecca, who hushed out, "James, excuse yourself for bringing the topic to the table."

Then Mr. Deacon stilled me. "Clara, please," he said as he nodded for me to stay in the room.

"I must not have made myself clear," he continued, "so I'll further the subject myself. Rigor mortis, they say. Already setting in by the time they found him ax-tight to his brother's porch a little after six o'clock a.m. The killer must have done his devil's work sometime around midnight, or shortly thereafter."

"Henry, dear, please," whispered Elizabeth.

"My point, in my own home, and at my own table, will be learned at least by my own friends."

"He's most correct, Mrs. Deacon," entered the good reverend. "If we can't recognize it as coincidence, then how can we expect the authorities to do the same?"

Then Benjamin Mason relaxed in his seat. "Yes, the connection they cling to is all I fear they're looking at. Perhaps all they've got. Take that first fellow, that Horace Wills." Then he looked to me, sad but determined, and said, "Beg my pardon,

Clara, but talk has it," as he looked back to the others, "and reasonable talk too, that he's of a cast that's been wronging people near all his adult life about this valley, whether through slights of his own miserable character, or out and out dreadful crimes, of the likes I believe he involved himself with this dear woman before us."

James Snyder, fingering his thin mustache, agreed. "Here, here," he added, before taking the table himself. "And this other fellow, this Mr. Logan—"

"Rest his soul, rest his soul," whispered the reverend. "And may peace come to the man-child too."

"Of course, Reverend, of course," James acknowledged the reverend, then went on with, "The *Gazette* calls him 'a former local man.' Former? I present to this table that this man hasn't lived about these parts for over fifteen years, perhaps upwards of twenty. No one knows him, not truly, not even his own folks. And he may have been followed, or even traveling with one or more of his own sort that his own family knows nothing of."

Oh that young Mr. Snyder, he was so ready to steady himself amongst the older men as I commenced with my duties. "Why the constables themselves," he went on, "all seemed so certain that those killed, around here or anywheres, are usually acquainted with, or, more regularly, quite well known by their own killers."

I figured his silly wife to be so proud of him, for I heard her from my kitchen work, say, "Oh James, I do hope they're investigating that line of figuring. Perhaps you should mention that to someone, dear."

Well, with that, even I was a bit eased, in spite of my prior nervousness over the subject. And as I finished the clearing of the big table to serve up a fine dessert of tea, coffee and a nice spread of cakes, it seemed that all about the table lightened a good deal regarding their conversation and fellowship in general.

And as usual, as I attended to them, I was happy to listen in on the talk of the men as it went into days and times past, when our part of Pennsylvania was known as the black forest, from our own Susquehanna Valley up and across the north mountains, into the more level lands of southern New York State. Of course they talked of logging, and of the giant trees felled, lumbered off, ". . . for the cities of Camden, Philadelphia and Baltimore," claimed Mr. Mason. "Why, even turning up in the shipyards of Europe," he added, smoking at the table, hard at it, rich and thick with his pipe.

They talked of the large profits of the same lumbering companies, and of the growth of the Susquehanna Boom Company, which I suppose regulated that trade, but didn't dare ask. They talked of the lumbering men themselves, of their hard laboring in those forests, and of their lives about their camps. "Saddled to whiskey, fiddlers and superstitions," added Reverend Ashhurst. "In sore need of proper sermons, especially amongst the homesick, the youngsters off from their homes for their first times."

Even the recent killings worked their way back into the men's conversation, but without need to check toward me, least not that I took note of. The topic resumed courtesy of young James Snyder, "Possibly a crazed logger, with a madness beyond all understanding."

Mr. Deacon figured this possible. "Lumbering's slowing considerable," he said as he chewed at his pipe, "leaving the excess, the unfit, to wander off, aimless amongst our own settled-in lives."

But the notions of days past wouldn't rest, and I felt it too, for my own girlhood was amongst that time of the busiest of the lumbering. The men talked of ghost tales and legends, and of the crudest of backwoods dentistry, and, as if the killings wouldn't entirely give way, circus life came up. "A way of life all its own," offered Mr. Mason.

"A company in and of itself," returned Mr. Deacon, "No less on wheels. And profitable to be sure, taxing people's need to be entertained. Different from what they've become used to."

"But dark people," studied the good reverend. "Sailors upon the land, I say. Souls without rightful places to claim as home. It's unnatural, you see."

"Forgive me," Rebecca Snyder chimed in smartly, "but you preach of shepherds, you do, who roam as well."

The reverend smiled. "Upon their own lands. It's righteous, my dear, to tend to one's own flock for seasonal fleecing, while guarding and caring over its needs. Circuses simply fleece, Mrs. Snyder, caring nothing for the pastures they cross, nor the flocks they happen upon."

"Well said, Reverend," smiled Mr. Mason. "But big out-fittings nonetheless. I understand they have their own barbers, carpenters, pay clerks, chain of labor and what else have you."

But lumbering too, refused to give entirely away, for it was our valley's other way of life. And as I kept to my responsibilities, I thought of how Joseph Logan never took to it, trying out his, by then, murdered brother's traveling show for a spell back then, just prior to my own dark days. And as I thought on while tending to the men, I listened in on topics of ". . . the times before these modern days of ours . . ." from Mr. Deacon, answered by the good reverend with, ". . . simpler times, poorer to be sure, but simpler and righteous . . ." reflected with, ". . . prior to this current, troubling immigration." Mr. Mason reminisced, "Peaceable days, such as those of our own Tom Sawyers and Huck Finns."

And then those two caught on, and I have to tell of them, for they'd catch on to myself as well, taking me in a quiet, seizing-me kind of way.

The person of Huckleberry Finn was the one they most earnestly discussed and worried over, for the story of his own mystery remained unchallenged by logging and circuses about the Deacons' table for a nice bit.

James Snyder was confident. "I tell you all, he died of the dysentery, in New Orleans, or St. Louis. I thought everyone knew it."

"No, dear, New Orleans is where he killed a man," his swollen bride assured him. "Before he vanished, on the run. I don't know anything about St. Louis."

Mr. Mason was quick. "Now I heard he vanished all right, and after killing someone, but it was out in San Francisco, and he didn't, my distinguished friend, vanish to ride with the Sioux against Custer and his boys," he warmly teased toward his host,

Mr. Deacon, who must have thought, or said as much at one time or another, for Mr. Deacon did smile back.

Then Elizabeth Deacon joined in, so I listened good.

"Well, Mr. Samuel Clemons himself says so little, you know," she addressed the whole table, "and I also heard that he, well, Mr. Clemons, that is," she smiled, "bought a farm right north of the mountains, up in New York State, near Elmira. Could you imagine that, living there with such a famous person about?"

But the good Reverend Ashhurst, kneading his bony hands, appeared solemn as he spoke his first on the matter. "He killed a boy. It was a boy, not a man, learned people have it. And out near Cincinnati. The *Herald* out there printed up their own accounting of the sordid business. It was just a boy. The boy of a strange woman he took up with. Not much else is known."

Mrs. Mason, ordinarily too quiet, broke the silence. "Congressman Sawyer, I've heard, says he may be dead or he may be alive, but either way he's still out there somewhere along that big muddy river. And if he is alive, he's no doubt a drunkard, as his father was. The congressman says his boyhood friend couldn't have known any other way," she said sadly.

"As for the honorable congressman, Tom Sawyer, now he did right well for himself," Mr. Deacon confirmed for the table. "What's he serving, his third or fourth consecutive term in the United States House?"

Mr. Mason smiled broad, exhaling some of his nice blue-gray smoke. "He didn't hurt himself getting the railroad to junction track on two of his own property holdings."

Mr. Deacon agreed, and so did young James, of course, as they talked on about the two boys, long since men by then, if the one was still alive. You see, one was real and rich with fame and power, as the other, the Finn boy, was by then lost to legend, and a popular topic of speculation, sometimes sad, sometimes cruel.

But it was their mentioning of railroading that sent myself quiet, adrift about my duties, recalling, I suppose, what I learned of it from Mr. Finley, from our few talks that I was beginning to miss by then. I thought of the shinplasters they got paid with from the pay car that came about, and of their "48 buckets" they ate from, being out for several days on end. Then I snapped awake, listening hard from my work in the kitchen for what I thought was a mentioning of Mr. Finley himself.

And indeed it was, for another one came, from the warmth of Mr. Mason's agreeable talk, from through the sweet smell of one of his grayish veils of smoke. "Well, Henry," he said, "I'll tell you what, just ask your man, Hank Finley. His name sounds near the same, now doesn't it?" he finished with a laugh.

They were back to the boys, the congressman and the legend. But I, myself, thought off again, on my own. And I ran both names by, several times through my mind. "Huck Finn—Hank Finley," and save me, they did indeed both sound near the same.

CHAPTER 7

Over a fortnight had passed, for it was late in April before I'd be close to kind old Mr. Finley once again.

Nothing else happened regarding either of the killings, save for the *Gazette* running several stories, one of which was accompanied with a photograph of Charlie with his circus somewhere. It was a bit blurred, but him to be sure, staring back at the camera. Regardless, I calmed considerable. I thought a good deal, but prayer soothed me as mere straight thinking dashed away most of my other frets.

In that time I was mainly about the spring-cleaning of the big house, tending to one musty room at a time. On one particular day it was Sarah's room, for I can recall her two rugs, hung after beating, after which Mr. Finley and myself dared a play of croquet, which was set up upon the opposite side of the big house, not far from my boiling-down lye for a fresh batch of soap cakes, which the farm was low on. I wished at the time that I was wearing a corset, or at least some hip padding to appear more ladylike. You see, in spite of my fears and concerns over him, and over my own self, I must have been a bit smitten, but I showed it none.

That particular evening, Mr. Finley himself was summoned to Mr. Deacon's office, a room kept closed off from the parlor. It seemed that Mr. Finley was working himself more and more into Mr. Deacon's favor. At least the farmhand talk had it that way. In any event, such a time we'd have, up until the end that is. And as it turned out, Mr. Finley did receive instructions from Mr. Deacon, regarding the seeding of the north fields, which spread out far from the farm, opposite the Mill Stream and northward. Apparently Henry Deacon was pleased with all the fields that spring having already been turned by plow. To move on, though, the children too were out upon the lawn, Sarah and her little brother, Joshua, two youngsters from town and my own Emma, when Mr. Finley crossed the big yard, where he paused and horsed with the one boy from town. Then he took notice of myself. And I waved, almost accidentally, you see, a touch embarrassing for myself.

Well, in that way of his, beneath the brim of his hat, his bony grin that needed a shave coaxed me from my boiling down of lye, which was in a heating-up waiting anyway. And he got me to take up a mallet, to play the first half through. I recall his balls being red, and my own playing before him, so mine had to be blue of course, due to turns. I also recall the grass being cool and thick, so it must have been high for croquet. But the Deacons' wickets were of heavy iron, and we of course, that Mr. Finley and myself, happy to play.

I was nervous at first, which is why I took to the subject of his railroading, for before he spoke so easy on it. And speak he did, for by the time we were angling in on the fifth wicket, in his studying way of play, he was telling me, "Brakemen and firemen are lower paid than the engineers and conductors, who mostly owned their own homes somewheres, as opposed to being renters."

I remained mostly quiet and listening, playing beside him. "So there's a difference between them?" I braved, "In station?"

"Not always, Miss Clara. Sometimes it were no matter," he said as he studied a bonus stroke in a weedy spot. "For such work is journeying work. And a body can be foolhearty when far from his family. I known right well fellers who weren't but firemen, yet owned finer homes than some of their own conductors."

Oh me oh my, I must have been soft for his southern way of talk, for I took to playing the game out, and I also took no pity rounding the ninth wicket, where my second ball nudged one of his own. I drove it off good, you see, with a whack and a smile for my first bonus stroke, and by about my second, my continuation stroke, we were on the subject of our town's namesake.

"We're named after the long gone Indian guide, and interpreter, Andrew Montour," I told him.

But Mr. Finley took a better interest in Andrew's mother, who I must have slipped in, that mysterious, at least to me, Madam

Montour. "She once lived about our Loyalsock Creek, and their Indian village of Otstonwakin," I told him.

Smiling for me, but not at me, Mr. Finley was downright interested as I told what little I knew of her as a large, regal sort of woman, of mixed blood, a daughter or a granddaughter of a French officer.

"I do believe that, Miss Clara. Probably a lot of that business goin' 'round back then." He steadied his way out of his ninth wicket jam.

I also told him of their village, called Otstonwakin, down at the mouth of the creek, which was, people claimed, back then farther downriver, though I didn't know how that could be, and said so.

He took me back a bit with, "Oh, Miss Clara, I been about rivers and creeks near all my life. Over time, they snakes about in awful pretty ways. Do believe me, ma'am."

Anyway, we wondered over Madam Montour, and I was happy, you see, to be talking so. And I believe we trailed off her just as real life had, her in defeat and defiant about it, having lost a favored son to warfare with whites, and then with her being somehow involved with the famous Wyoming massacre off east in coal country, and then her hiding about in her old age and sullen majesty.

Mr. Finley then stood tall, suspending his game, quieting himself. "I feel for her, Miss Waltz. I truly do. Folks can be cruel to one another. They truly can."

As we neared the game's end, Mr. Finley did gain on me considerable, and he brightened with our talk of loggers and log drivers, especially regarding their run-ins with the rafters, who felt the river more rightfully theirs. I found that curious with my silly wonderings, of course, but I wouldn't be shaken until our cleaning up of our contest, prior to my returning to my soap-cake making.

The young ones had gone off by then, I believe, to Mill Creek to play until sundown, as it was their habit then. It must have been raining good out over the road to Muncy, for a thick, pretty rainbow arched out high into the dark business of the eastern sky. And it was then that a new warmth came over me for that older-than-me Mr. Finley, for his happiness over the rainbow.

"It's God's good promise to not flood the world again for our earthly ways," I told him.

But Mr. Finley thought different, and told me so. "Oh, Miss Clara, I heard tell of it," as his unshaven face stared off to the colors of the sky, "and I do believe it to be so, that it's light breakin' or bendin' or something of that nature, through the rain-drops still in the sky. But the angle's got to be correct. See, the sun's got to be opposite in the sky." He pointed. "And you can see she is now, settin' in the west behind us. If I had a stick and some dirt beneath us I could draw it out for ya."

"If that were so, Mr. Finley, then the whole beautiful promise would have to be falling just as the rain out there is," I cor-rected him.

"No ma'am, I was told that the whole thing is flickering, only so fast and so far off, she looks steady to us. It's that angle thing as the rain falls through her."

And then I did it, and I'll never know why. It just sprung from me, like a schoolgirl.

"Were you ever married, Mr. Finley?" I asked him, the both of us still staring at God's good work in the sky.

If he was took back he showed it none, but I was, so I added quick, "I don't mean to be fresh, sir. I'm sorry." And it came from me humble too.

"Don't be. Don't be, Miss Waltz," he said, gazing to the sky.

And then he went on, as though it felt good for him to do so. He answered me, out loud to himself. Like a pain, it did seem to me, for that was something I knew of.

"I was with a woman once. A woman I was right fond of for quite a stretch," he said sad-like, around a working of his big Adam's apple that could have used a shave as I said before. "I weren't ever betrothed to her though. Wouldn't hear of it. Her, ma'am, that is. A right tall woman she was too. So tall she hunched herself to hide it, I were certain at times. Mean too," he smiled then, but only briefly, "to near all 'cepting her boy. She had a son, lil' Robbie. He wasn't mine, Miss Waltz." He looked to me quick. "A nice little boy he was too, with big bucked teeth that coulda, well—well, he's gone now. Passed away."

That scared me. A dead boy and all, so I told him, "You needn't go on with it, Mr. Finley, if it pains you."

"It's all right, Miss Clara," he sighed. "It was all a long time ago, and she herself is probably gone now too. She was gravely ill last I ever saw of her. Gravely ill, Miss Clara," he said as he turned away, maybe to hide thickening eyes beneath that weathered hat, for his voice sounded so.

I might also add, and I do hope it doesn't sound most queer, but even through my fear then, I do recall that conversation as the second time I smelled of Mr. Finley's closeness, even as the names spun in my head—Hank Finley, Huckleberry Finn—Hank Finley, Huck Finn, that smell came rich to me through the air. I couldn't recall the first time, nor can I still. Perhaps it was upon the wagon that time he brought me home from Mrs. Snyder's. But that very same richness remains dear to me even now.

* * *

Then heavy rains returned to our valley. Oh me oh my, they were dark and gray and constant, and almost warm, falling upon our times back then. The logs ran too, in record numbers, Mr. Deacon said, since the flood of the year before. What a sight to see, down the creeks and out upon the rising Susquehanna. And folks visited the banks of the waters just to take in the sight of all the logs, and the rafters working their loads through the rain. The children, in slickers, often stayed and played upon the soaked banks until nightfall, and I too managed to slip down to our own covered bridge that crossed the Loyalsock, bound for Williamsport, to have a look for Emma's sake. All was proud I suppose.

Of course the rafters and the loggers watched the water's depth by the day, and by the inches, waiting for the call for the logs to run hard, down from our mountains and away from our valley. But there were other workings of the inch by inch kind as well, and they must have bottomed themselves out in shallower waters, for one afternoon brought lawmen through the rain to the Deacons' big fine house, that Deputy Constable Keeler from Williamsport, and our own Constable Amos Reese.

They wouldn't question me there, though, not in the Deacons' parlor that I warmed with a low coal fire to dry the house air. This time they saddled me up on the old bay and led me up into town, to the borough office, the back part of it, which was Amos' office. I also took notice that Amos stayed quiet and steadfast through the rain, never looking to me as we rode up onto Broad Street, through the handful of crossings that was our town back then. I didn't know if he decided himself, or was told to, but he seemed firm on a side, and I didn't blame him for he had duties of his own, just as the Williamsport men had, all of them hard on their search.

And I feared, I did, wishing the ride were longer, and I didn't know if it was wrong of me, but I fancied Mr. Finley's being about, somewhere unseen, bearing witness to my being led off for another's wrongs. And even more wrong was my own determination upon that wet ride to lie through two truths, one easy and pure, for I truly knew nothing of how Charlie Logan was killed. But that first murdering remained with me, incomplete, but with me nonetheless. You see, I never saw Horace Wills die. I did find him dead, and I saw the last two people he saw, and I heard some of his last words, for they were about me, but I never watched him die, and I would cling to that if I had to. Perhaps I was being true to that queer man, Mr. Hank Finley, or perhaps it was some other justice I wished to belong to.

Upon entering Amos' office, I saw that they had it prepared for me, and that frightened me. They had an electric lamp so the dark room lit up quick. Three more men stood about the room. They were that silent other deputy constable from Williamsport, and our own deputies, Harold Elmer, who looked scared, and Amos' handsome son-in-law, John Thomas Moon, who rose to greet me, all wet himself, taking my wraps. Then he directed me to a lone chair against the one wall, as all else settled in.

Little was said at first, as the wetness seemed to follow us into the room in damp tracks, and then in dripping little pools that grew beneath the hung wraps.

Big Amos Reese spoke first.

"Clara, we brung you here because we just aren't certain you were entirely on the level with us before," he began as he paced before me.

The others watched on, save for that Constable Keeler, who then slid a table before me, as if I was to be fed alone, for no other chairs were brought up. Then, with no help from the others, oh me oh my, did he ever lay into me, at first measured and direct, and then wild and fearful, at least for me.

"You know, Clara Waltz, Miss Clara Waltz, some minds hold that women, women such as yourself, that is," he said, "are apt to lie about anything to further their own ends in general." And then he hollered, straight into my face, "God damn you, you liar!"

I jumped in my chair, and looked about. None other moved.

"Look to me, God damn you!" he demanded.

I obeyed.

"I'm going get to the truth of what you know, woman, if I have to keep you here before me all this god-damned rainy day!"

And then he yelled again, "Can you hear me?! Do you hear me, woman?! I want the truth!" as he clung tight to my table, his hair wet, his eyes locked to my own.

"Yes. Yes, I hear you." I tried to check my shaking, as my eyes thickened with tears.

And then he hollered some more. "I can't stand women such as you! No one can. Living with people as fine as the Deacons! It's an unfitfulness overlooked!" Then he shouted even louder, wild-eyed like a creature, "We want the killer!"

"I don't know your truth," I said. Then wishing to plead I added his name. "Mr. Keeler, sir." Then softly, and half believing it myself, I told him, "Perhaps it's the avenge of Jehovah."

From Isaiah I offered to all in the room, for I feared looking at Constable Keeler, "From 1:24, I think: 'Therefore the utterance of the Lord, Jehovah of armies, I shall relieve myself of my adversaries, and I will avenge myself on my enemies to those who have become partners with thieves.' "

"This is your answer?" shouted Mr. Keeler.

"I have done nothing," I kept on, "and I don't know why what is happening is happening." I strengthened with that part of the truth. "I too have wondered long and fearfully over this. Perhaps it's our Lord." I began to weep. "But it's not me. Perhaps a man sent to me, or to all of us."

"He's a killer!" the constable screamed at me, "not a god-damned angel! What in hell is wrong with you?" as he banged two-fisted upon the table.

Then he calmed, and leaned over that very table, the only thing that separated us. "You must agree, Miss Waltz, you must agree with us on this single point. And another thing, let's leave the Good Book out of this, shall we?"

I must have nodded, for he pushed on.

"These are modern times, Miss Waltz," he said with a quirk of a smile, staying so close to me. "The railroad connects the entire country, and they're laying new track by the day. In what, only ten, fifteen years now, phonographs in most homes, telephones in near every important building. Modern times, Miss Waltz. Electric lamps." He nodded to the one burning in the corner. "Carbon filament they call it. Reckoned to be in most decent homes by the turn of the century." Then he leaned closer. "Modern times, Clara Waltz." I was against the wall, and I couldn't lean back. I could see the veins in his eyes as he told me, "We aim to get this killer with modern ways."

"I understand, Mr. Keeler. Constable Keeler."

"That's better," he breathed at me without blinking, which I don't know why I noticed. "Now, let's start again, way back, with things you surely know of by your own word. Now, you've claimed, ten or eleven years ago—"

"Nearly twelve, sir. It was nearly twelve years ago."

"Fine, Miss Waltz. Mighty fine. So, nearly twelve years ago you say five men took a, well, an excess to your most private womanly self. Did you willingly partake in this perverse adventure?"

I looked about. The others waited. I could hear the rain outside. And then I did it. I started to cry, the choking, hard to breathe sort.

"I said before that I didn't ever wish to talk of the matter anymore. I said that back—"

"Robbed you!" he hollered at me. "Clean robbed you of your very own female treasure was your tale of despair and accusation," he continued, as he again banged upon the table. "And now, Miss Waltz, now they seem to be dying. Two of those five! No coincidence, I propose and I maintain!"

I nearly whispered, "I know nothing."

He bore in on me, "Well, one of those very men, those evil men of yours, tried to extend a genuine kindness to you, he claims, only a month ago."

My thoughts and such scrambled up quick, for I didn't know what he was talking about.

"Oh my, Miss Waltz. Come now, a fine and reputable farmer of down Montgomery way, and you had nothing but spite and vengeance for him as he tried to be decent to you."

I must have honestly looked confused, for he leaned closer, following with, "Come now, before a crowd up in the Market Street Square. One of Mr. Deacon's own hands was there with you. That Finley fellow. Shall I have a talk with him as well?"

"If you wish so. I do recall that incident now," I wept. Through my weeping I added, "I have no interest in Mr. Kremer's interests. I know nothing else."

"Oh, you remember now. I see." Then he spun fast to the others, pointing back at my tearful self and added, "Furthering her own ends!"

Then he turned back to me, and hissed through his tightened face, "You're a liar, and a waste of any decent man's time. You're a wretched thing. A shame to good people, and a menace to all. Two dead in two months. We law-abiding folks can expect another killing in what, three or four weeks or so?"

Then he looked at the floor and spat, and said to me without looking up, "I have to get away from your kind. You sicken me, Miss Waltz. I'll be back, and we'll have another try at this."

He turned to the silent others. "Let's go, men, for coffee and some meal. The air's too foul in here for an honest soul. Deputy Moon, stay with her and see she doesn't leave that table. You'll take no statements from her, you hear?"

"Yes, sir," Amos' son-in-law snapped.

Then Constable Keeler and the rest were out the door, into the rain, leaving only the buzz of that electric lamp, and me and Deputy Constable John Thomas Moon left in that room.

* * *

The four were gone near half the hour before Deputy Constable Moon spoke to me.

"Miss Waltz, ma'am? Would you take a tea or a coffee?"

I said nothing, so he waited, then repeated himself.

"I don't think we're permitted to speak," I whispered.

"He'll never know. A drink would be good for you."

Then Mr. Moon left the room and returned quickly with two hot cups from somewhere, placing one before me as he slid his own chair up to my table.

He winced from the heat of his own coffee, before telling me softly, "You took a sound questioning, Miss Waltz."

I stayed silent, fearful of the return of the others.

"You needn't fear me, Miss Clara. We've known each other for several years now."

"How long will he keep me here, Mr. Moon?" I braved.

"Tommy, please. You can call me Tommy. I go by that. And I don't rightly know, Miss Clara. I reckon for another effort at it anyway. I'm really less than a deputy. I'm part time. I work out at the paper mill. Out Loyalsock Avenue."

"I know that."

"Well, I don't know, at least in detail or anything, what the Williamsport men, or Amos either, already knows, or for what they're after. Besides the killer, of course."

Then he sipped his coffee and gave me a sad smile, and he was indeed as handsome as they all agreed. "That Keeler fellow, he was dead right about one thing, Miss Waltz. Things round here, and all over everywhere, they are changing. You're about my age, aren't you?"

"Be thirty-one come next fall," I answered, easing up a good measure.

"Twenty-nine years myself," he spoke, seeming to relax himself.

Then, all alone, save ourselves, we did have ourselves a nice chat, with him doing near all the talking, of course.

He told me of his boyhood swimming holes along the Loyalsock Creek, under the covered bridge and at points I knew of along the canal. And he told me of the canal's muddy waters and of catfishing the bottoms for the evening meals. This caused me to reflect on my own Emma, and of her own growing up so fast around our town, just as it made me think of my own spent youth, up Lycoming Creek, which I mentioned.

He brightened. "Tell me of it, Miss Clara. I'd like to hear it."

I told some, but shied considerable when he laughed so at a bad cold and a boil that kept me out of the water.

"Lycoming Creek, huh?" he asked. "A nice heavy stream, most like our own Loyalsock." And at another point it was, "Cogan Station, huh? Never been there. Can you believe that?"

"I can, sir. It wasn't, and still isn't the growing town such as Montoursville is." Why Montoursville must have had two hundred homes by then, and I told him that. "Cogan Station, Mr. Moon, is more a stopoff, northbound out of Williamsport, before the mountains get thick."

Then Deputy Constable Moon slipped back easily into his boyhood, as men can do, and I didn't mind listening. It was the killing of the wild pigeons, and it was a pretty spin, for I recalled our own springtime nettings of the pigeons as they flew north every spring for the beech forests of our mountains. His handsome face softened as he spoke of the great flocks that flew cloudlike, over Bald Eagle Mountain. His mentioning of that mountain of course returned my own thoughts to Stacy Kremer, but not for long, as Mr. Moon reflected on the shootings, the trappings and the joyous nettings of the passenger pigeons, which was indeed calming to listen to.

"You know, Clara," he seemed to think aloud, "One's hard pressed to see but a dozen of 'em anymore."

"I know," I answered him, sipping from my cooling coffee.

"Some say there just ain't many of 'em left. What do you figure?"

"I don't know. I too remember the big flocks, like clouds of birds."

"They're just somewhere else is all. Flying to somewhere else," he said, seeming to be finished with it, for then he looked at me and asked me, "Are you feeling better? You know, the tears and all?"

"Yes, I am. Thank you."

"I don't like all the yelling, and of course the tears. I truly don't," he said so honestly.

And then we talked of the spring freshets and of the log runnings, of those past, and of the one going on. This caused me to look to the window. The rain had stopped, but the sky remained gray and moving. This turned me to worrying over the return of the others, for near an hour had passed. But Mr. Moon wished to talk of the spring planting, to begin in a week or so.

"Us boys and girls," he went on, "back as kids, we marched in our lines a yard apart, dropping the grains where the furrows met up with one another, all across those big fields. You ever do it as a child, Miss Clara?"

"A few times," I answered, "but we didn't like the dirt."

"We did. When I was a boy we abandoned our shoes and stockings for the warm soft earth, we did. And every now and again one of us would happen upon an arrowhead. Once, little Jeffrey—Jeffrey Bolen—you know him?"

"Just of him is all."

"Well, once he found himself a pipe, he did. Probably still has it somewhere," he said before going on about how they got paid fifty cents per day in shinplasters.

"And we saved it all too, Miss Clara. Most all anyways, in keen anticipation of the summer circus." He smiled toward the ceiling.

And that, the notion of the big show, must have brought him to it.

"Due to roll in, in late June, without that Charlie Logan fella', Miss Clara," he commented softly.

I stayed quiet myself, truly thinking of the great train of the circus itself, steaming in, over a mile long.

"Can you tell me, Clara?" Handsome John Thomas Moon leaned to me, and added quietly, "Can you tell me anything? I can help you. Honest, I can."

Oh me oh my, he seemed so concerned and caring over me, and it was so tempting to relieve myself of my pain.

"It's us against them, Clara. Can't you see that? Them Williamsport men don't know us folks. They want anyone, and I'll wager a month's work they got nothing. Nothing at all."

"Then why me, Mr. Moon? Why me?"

"Cause they got themselves a coincidence, Miss Clara, which is nothing at all. Let me help you," he hushed out, reaching to me, touching my hand. "I can help you. Just between me and you. I won't breathe a word. If'n there's anything at all you can tell me, I can get'cha out of this fix you're in."

Oh, how the buzz of that electric light did drill into me, and Constable Moon's handsomeness, and the moving gray sky through the window as I looked about, frightened and tempted.

"You don't want Keeler screamin' at you all over again, do you?" he pleaded quietly, leaning in on me, his handsomeness close to me.

I reflected upon the croquet, and upon that wagon ride, and upon what I did and did not see from within that hollow log.

"I know nothing. Nothing at all, Mr. Moon. Just confusion is all. I can tell you, though, I can't feel any proper remorse for those two men, and I pray for myself over it, but only on that account, for as a Christian I truly should.

And then I quieted, listening to my own heart, and to the breathing of Amos' son-in-law, and then to that electric lamp as well. I don't know why I didn't tell what I didn't tell. I suppose it was for Mr. Finley's ever kindness. Even from that first time I ever saw him, it was a kindness upon that frozen riverbank. Sinful and savage, but in its waiting way it was a kindness to me.

Then the next thing I knew the other four men entered, so I braved myself up. But only big Amos Reese spoke.

"You can be on your way, Clara. Go on and go home, and we thank you for your time."

I rose from behind my table. Deputy Constable Keeler stared mean at me as I gathered myself up, getting my wraps from Harold Elmer, who cloaked me softly, as though I might break.

* * *

Outside, it was trying to rain again, but the sky just couldn't. I also didn't mount the old bay. I just walked her home through a moving, damp mist, not wanting to put the load of myself upon her as we made our way toward the Loyalsock, and the Deacons' fine big house, which wouldn't seem to be mine anymore, nor ever truly would again.

* * *

I'm near certain it was that same night, for I was pretty shook, and I do know it was some time after Emma turned toward me in her sleep that I found in Paul to the Romans, in the seventh chapter, some timely wisdom concerning widowhood and the laws of wives to their husbands. I read on, then stayed with the latter part of 7:3, the end of it to be true: ". . . but if her husband dies, she is free from his law, so that she is not an adulteress if she becomes another man's."

Oh, how I truly felt a terrible and a certain changing about me. And I prayed too, that it would be a good thing for me, for I felt as though I was somehow being set free from those men who married me into the life mine had become.

I wondered if it was my Lord, or if it was only that Mr. Hank Finley, just a man. And then I wondered who he really was, for I just didn't know.

But I also couldn't help returning to the truth. Both were killings, you see. Murderings.

Oh, they were awful ponderings about that changing time of mine, that time that I felt as though I was somehow being set free. But it still hurt, it did.

CHAPTER 8

Those April rains passed, then more came and then they too passed, as with most of that April, and I suppose, as with the suspicions that surrounded myself back then. And I was content about that, for I had enough to concern myself over with the spring-cleaning near halfway done.

Of course the Deacons went on entertaining their guests, and Emma and I, with Elizabeth a touch picky, went on putting those nice spreads upon their table. About one, hosting Samuel and Ellen Wills, I learned that Constable Keeler traveled again, to Trenton, New Jersey, to meet with the traveling circus people themselves as their show worked its way about. I never heard anything of what he come back with, but I saw no more of him nor his silent partner, which was fine by me. I also don't believe the subject held what it once had, for the talk about the Deacon table gave way easy to their common enough gold over silver standard quarreling, and other such matters which may have concerned them directly or not.

As for Emma, I guessed these things didn't shake her as I thought and feared. She and Sarah Deacon even warmed a bit to one another, much like they had when they were just little things, for as I said before, Emma was, of course, of a different station so to speak. But young Sarah, especially if the Rakestraw twins, Allison and Alexandra, weren't about, was more than kind to my Emma. She even gave her clothes on occasion, mostly loose wraps and such, but nice articles just the same. She also gave Emma her dime novels once she was done with them. They were all over back then, the Horatio Alger rags-to-riches tales, and those Beadle Dime Novels of the great out west, one of which was my own favorite, #45 or such, titled *Esther: A Story of the Oregon Trail*. I sneaked it around my duties and was even caught at it by Elizabeth Deacon, who told me, with a smile, that she too read a few herself. Anyway, it did my heart good, for Emma did wish so to be like Sarah Deacon. What little girl wouldn't?

As for myself, I still felt my changing, but it became a slower thing, I suppose. After the planting ended, I also got to see more of Mr. Hank Finley about the big house, but to that later. To myself, I just watched things closer and thought about my circumstances and myself in a different light so to speak. For instance, when up in Williamsport for a stay with ailing Mrs. Snyder, I found myself caring different for her, more tender and more honest about that duty. When relieved by Rebecca on my third day, I couldn't concern myself with her Joseph Logan news, or meddling, that she was so earnest to tell of.

"I learned, through James," she told me, "that Joseph too has been questioned, and rigorously as well. And a good deal of their questioning was time spent over what he knows of you."

"I don't care, Rebecca," I dared using her first name. "He only knows one thing about me."

But Rebecca went on, and Joseph Logan had lied of course, to a lesser wrong, but I wouldn't favor Rebecca with it. Her husband, James, had it that Joseph claimed that he and the others had themselves some drunken sport with me, no more than that, rough and unkind perhaps, but not near the lies, he claimed to that Constable Keeler, that I came up with way back then.

"Well, perhaps that's what's taking them off you, Clara," Rebecca said smartly. "Why would one kill and murder and such over the drunken horseplay of grown men so long ago? At least according to James and Harold Elmer."

I only listened, supposing to myself that Harold Elmer was probably all certain and brave about it too, safely far off from any of the doings over it. But you see, as Rebecca went on, so sure she was doing me some sort of goodwill, I truly had to try to listen to her, for my thoughts were more about poor Mrs. Snyder, sitting there between us, in her own parlor, staring off at nothing. In those visits of caring for her that spring, I took a quiet interest in her poor soul, which laid so still within her somewhere, behind her cloudy eyes that didn't seem to see a thing.

In cleaning, I went more thorough, as though her home were the Deacons'. And in doing so, I came across some of her old schoolgirl things, saved-away readers and spellers along with two, yellowed with age, arithmetic ledgers. I learned her maiden name, and thought it rung pretty as I repeated it to her as I spooned her her broth, and as I washed her for her bed. One evening I read from her big Bible instead of from my own, and in leafing about I came upon her family tree, of which I asked her about the next day, and talked to her about, keeping the both of us company.

Of course she never spoke from her staring off, but the point was myself. I was gaining a new faith, a new way about my world then, and I began to see this better when I shared Mrs. Snyder's Bible with Rebecca when she came. All Rebecca could do, swollen with her own child, was deny the testaments in favor of the family tree.

She snickered over the dates of the poor old woman's first-born, "Birthed just six months after her marriage, Clara. So much for James' perfect mother, I tell you. Humph!"

I said nothing, for I had my Emma, and no husband at all.

"Oh, don't be so stiff. Have a little fun, and grow up," she told me.

But my own eyes, you see, had wandered about that family tree, off to Mrs. Snyder's third born, lost in three days. And I thought about the difference between what people do for show, and what people do for love. The next time the duty was mine, I'd tell poor Mrs. Snyder, as silent as she was, of my own lost child.

And as to Mr. Hank Finley, back then, after my second questioning, he just stayed his tall and thin, good-natured self. I recall well the events of that early May, and I duly shall, but as for the times of the end of that April, I have to search a bit harder, not so much for the events, but for the order of their occurrence.

It was towards that April's end that Mr. Finley first dined with the Deacons, all proper-like in their dining room, with Emma and I of course at their waiting. Henry Deacon claimed the invite was only fitting, for such a fine turning of the fields, and for such a timely sowing of possibly the biggest crop yet to yield. "Handsomely improved upon . . ." were Mr. Deacon's own words.

Reverend Ashhurst dined alongside, along with Benjamin and Sarah Mason. The good reverend, of course, gave the blessing and spared me that time, never mentioning any talk of crimes or criminals about. Mr. Finley would ask me a few days later, though, "Why do you suppose it is that folks' voices change so when they pray?"

"Why, how do you mean, Mr. Finley?" I asked.

"Why, ma'am, all the 'seethes,' 'thous,' and 'mayeths,' and what have you. Such is Bible talk, a body would reckon."

"He's truly a religious man is all, if you're asking of Reverend Ashhurst."

"Just seems peculiar to me, Miss Clara. Perhaps the Maker and Jesus do appreciate it though. I suppose they do indeed."

But back to that nice dining, with Mr. Finley in attendance, the only mentioning of the killings was Mr. Mason's sharing with the table Constable Keeler's travels, this time, to Scranton, to question the circus people again regarding Charles Logan's death. I imagined his silent friend to be with him, but none mentioned him. I also took notice that Mr. Finley never so much as flinched to the subject. He just ladled himself a fresh heaping of gravy is all.

Then just days later, I received a letter from that Stacy Kremer. A very kind and considerate note, asking if I'd meet with him, for he was very concerned with ". . . the recent developments which brought Williamsport constables to my peaceful farm . . ." I declined by never answering his letter. I did, though, share it with Elizabeth Deacon, allowing her to read it as well, for I never received postage, you see, and I was sure she was curious, especially about those times. I wanted to tell Hank Finley of it too, but couldn't. I nearly did, near the first of May when we had ourselves a nice talk while walking up into town for separate purchases. We chatted of birds, of the robins that arrived in black clouds every spring, to leave late each fall, for a smaller flock wavered off in the sky before us.

"To avoid the winter," I told him.

"I once heard right sensible talk though, Miss Clara, that they never saw a winter, nor are they smart enough to think one over, so their coming and going in mass just works out for them thisaway," he said as he pondered those birds and the blue sky, walking beside me.

"The Good Lord's work, Mr. Finley, shouldn't be questioned by folks."

"Well," he said as he smiled truly, "I don't aim to offend anyone, 'specially the Maker. They are awful pretty, though, those big flocks."

That talk took me to John Thomas Moon's boyhood passenger pigeons, so I asked Mr. Finley of his thoughts.

"No ma'am, just gone, and not to somewhere else. Less of 'em is all," his bony face said sadly. "That's all there is to it. Less of 'em."

But he cheered up quick and considerable. He was like that, he was. Oh me oh my, how I wondered over him. What cheered him was my telling him of that Madam Montour, half-breed Indian woman, and then how the slaughter of white folks at the Battle of Wyoming Valley sent an unknown lone rider through our own valley, clean up Bald Eagle Ridge, over a hundred years before, when all was wilderness. I also began a tale of white women abducted by the savages, one I heard as a young girl up Lycoming Creek, to be made wives of, but he stopped me, for he didn't care to hear of, or ponder over, the notion of motherless children. He was a man, himself, to ponder over.

And it was about that time, I have to figure, that Elizabeth Deacon informed me that she and Mr. Deacon planned to take their family for a holiday, into the western mountains, up to Renova for a week that May. I could follow them, with Emma, or arrange plans of my own should I prefer to not accompany them. She added, though, that getting away myself might be helpful and prudent, considering the events of that spring

I did feel that need, but not with the Deacons, bless their kindness. Instead, I wrote to my father, up in Cogan Station, wishing to return to my girlhood home, just for a visit.

* * *

So that's what I set out to do, and I made my plans as I boiled down the new soap cakes for that May, for it was a lengthy chore, a waiting sort of work about one's kettles that allows a person to think of other things while the fats and the oils boil down five or six times.

And I decided, most contently, to be grand about it too, with new clothes for both Emma and myself. Renova, you see, wasn't for us. Snuggled up, northwest of us, deep in the forest beneath thousand-foot hills, I heard tell, it was the summertime health spot for the rich. No, Emma and I chose Cogan Station, the Little Bear Inn, for my father had answered my letter as I had answered Stacy Kremer's, with none at all.

And it did turn out to be something of a trip for us. We took the Catawissa to Williamsport, then the Northern, bound for Ralston and beyond. We departed, naturally, at Cogan Station, and there we stayed for all of three nights and four days. It doesn't seem much, I'm sure, just Emma and myself, but she was just at the right age to understand that I was once a young girl too.

It was a personal, rich time for us, it was, for Emma liked seeing the places where I played and swam with my sister. My father's home, of course, once mine, we kept a distance from, and that must have made it all the more mysterious to her little eyes, especially when I pointed out the windows of the room where she had come into this world.

At the Little Bear Inn we got silly full of ourselves, being waited on and all. And our room was nice too, all neat and kept for us. But most memorable to me now were our visits to Pastor English's church and home. He had aged so, much beyond the years that had passed, but his kindness to Emma and myself was as genuine as it was to myself a dozen years before, when he first allowed me to slip into the back of his church.

He and his wife welcomed us midday and unannounced. They also still kept after their little farm, but worked only hogs anymore, for the pastor claimed they weren't as hard to keep after, and then he laughed for Emma, telling her that they were mainly "the old woman's" pleasure anyway.

At his home, he told me how he heard talk of my own name being associated with the recent killings. He was caring, and cautious, with Emma present.

"She's aware, Pastor. She knows that I knew those two men," I assured him. "I was also hoping that up here, in Cogan Station anyway, that my name would be left out from that business."

"No, Clara, it wasn't. But folks are gentle with it, your name, that is." He sort of smiled. "You've been gone for some time, you know. So tell me," he changed the subject, "are those Deacons as good to you as that Reverend Ashhurst promised me they'd be?"

I assured him they were, as we talked on, with me not feeling like the harlot girl I had all those years before, because the pastor and his wife were good to us. At their table that evening the pastor read to us from Matthew, of Jesus' wishes for all, and I assumed for my own circumstances. I recall 5:44, "However, I say to you, continue to love your enemies and pray for those persecuting you, that you may prove yourselves sons of your Father who is in the Heavens." And I said the "Amen," for it mattered to me.

The good Pastor English walked with us too, and he took us about in his fine carriage, the very carriage Emma and I sadly rode nine years before, away from Lycoming Creek, with our two bags of all we owned when she was but three—on our way to meet the kind Deacons.

"Have you talked to your father, Clara?" Pastor English asked me.

"He won't have it, Pastor. I tried, through posted letter."

"I have good company then." He smiled to me. "He barely allows me on his porch, let alone inside for thoughtful talk."

Then we talked of the nature of forgiveness regarding my father, with the pastor reminding me that the both of us needed to attend to our own, for one another. My father for his disappointment in me, and mine for his abandoning me back then, and forever more it seemed. I recall now asking Mr. Finley, sometime later, of the same subject. He had a thought too.

"Miss Clara," he said to me as we walked, "it could be righteous, but I don't know much of righteous things. Forgiveness does, though, ma'am, forgiveness does, somehow mostly favor the forgiver in one way or another over the forgiven, while doing no harm to either of the concerned."

* * *

The Pastor English couldn't accompany us to Ellie's little grave, and it turned out nicer, I do believe.

On our long walk there, from the Little Bear Inn, I showed Emma more of where and of how I lived as girl. She was all eyes and ears to be so alone with me. And how she laughed so at my recalling how we teased kittens with the sunfish we caught, getting the kittens to climb us like trees as we held the fish high above us.

At the cemetery, though, she quieted, as I suppose I had too, especially at Ellie's grave. But hers may have been different. They say twins are curious things. But the graveyard was on high ground, and far we could see. I remember so well the hard breeze and the billowy whiteness of the clouds that day, for, you see, I got to looking at the hills and the mountains that surrounded us, and I pondered that early afternoon, what was beyond them, for it dawned on me strong that I myself had never ventured from our own valley. And then more thoughts swept through me, ones of Mr. Hank Finley, for he had come from beyond the mountains I surveyed. And then I felt a touch of shame for thinking of him as I had in that wind, as Emma poked about her sister's long grown-over grave. So I listened. My Emma was telling the cold stone a story, something about how she'd enjoy so sitting beside her in school. Yes, I do believe twins are curious things.

We'd pay visiting to the pastor's home once more after that, for supper and an evening of fellowship. Pastor English spoke again of my father, a tale of my father's from two summers before, of accidentally digging up dog bones off the back porch, opposite the outhouse, and my poor father couldn't recall which dog it could have been. I told the pastor it was Ashes, the smoky gray stray which took to us when I was just Emma's age, but I didn't mention my not understanding why my father couldn't recall it, not after the big event my sister made of it.

Before we parted, us for the Inn and the pastor to his life, Pastor English advised me of my own faith, for I asked him, "Any parting thoughts, Pastor English, for a lonesome woman?"

"James, Miss Waltz, as he sermoned to the Twelve Tribes in 1:26. Let me show you," he said as he spread and opened his big Bible. Then he read it out to me: " 'If any man seems to himself to be a formal worshipper, and yet does not bridle his tongue, but goes on deceiving his own heart, this man's worship is vain.'

"Don't deceive your own heart, Miss Waltz," he talked on, warmly and kindly, as I read the following verse, 1:27, silently to myself: "Pure religion before God and the Father is this, to visit the fatherless and the widows in their tribulation . . ." and the rest I trailed off from, thinking of him again, and I didn't feel shame for it that time either.

That night, in the quiet tidiness of our room at the Little Bear, I searched my Bible more as Emma slept beside me. I read late, and from both the Old and the New Testaments, but ended my Scriptures for the night in the second of Corinthians, with Paul's words of 6:14, "Do not become unevenly yoked with un-believers. For what fellowship do righteousness and lawlessness have? Or what sharing does light have with darkness?"

I turned down our wick after that, and took note of the cool breeze from the darkness outside, sweeping down through the valley. Then I prayed for Emma and myself, then for all else, and then more over him.

* * *

I did miss him. I do know that, for upon our return, and even after the return of the Deacons, I found myself having to be about outside more than my duties called for, and even about the big barn or any of the outbuildings, mostly having to show

Emma something or another. But it was easy, for he too, I took note, was about the big house more and more, and often for things any of the field help could have tended to. And with those times we managed to talk a bit when we could, but that wasn't it, save me. It was the smiles we traded, especially the ones from afar. You see, I wasn't used to feelings such as those.

Then, and never to be lost to me, come mid-May, I had to serve another of my turns with Mrs. Snyder. Mr. Finley was in the midst of five days' worth of hauling sold hay to a Williamsport buyer, to return with dung from the city's east end. I could have managed the Catawissa fare up, but of course I chose not to. I had it arranged that Mr. Finley, about his other duties, would take me to Williamsport, and return me home whenever I was to be relieved.

* * *

Mr. Finley hauled that hay and dung with the farm's big rigging, teamed to four of the workhorses, and we did, indeed, have ourselves a nice ride up, sharing the sleigh seat I told of earlier.

I told him of my recent fondness for poor old Mrs. Snyder, and he favored me with his admiration for that, which I felt true. Then he told me a tale, which made him happy to relate. He learned of it from one of the laboring hands of the Watsons' big farm down along the river, whose fields I crossed not five months before, in tears in the icy cold, though it mattered little to me then.

"Mr. Watson's man at the depot told me this feller was an Englishman, Miss Clara, somebody Silverman. And an odd feller he must a been, living down along the river about Sunbury, or Selinsgrove, and some years before," Mr. Finley went on.

Points south, I thought, where I've never been, but the tale so cheered Mr. Finley that I dared not interrupt.

"Well, apparently this feller lived out on the river herself, across a chain of islands between those two towns, and he right called himself, and asked to be addressed as, the 'Master of the

Seven Islands,' Miss Clara." Mr. Finley smiled broad. "Watson's man told me this feller paraded himself all grand in his style of clothes and his mannerings and such."

"How did he earn his keeping?" I asked, truly wondering.

"Sold shad. Mostly in the spring. And other fish too. They say he even gained himself a modest wealth, because he had no notes of debt to no one."

"Was he friendly?"

"Oh yes, if you didn't pay any mind to his carrying himself in his Lordly fashion, 'cause, as he claimed, all others was common." Mr. Finley smiled broad again, rewrapping the thick leather reins of the team. "Oh, Miss Clara," he told me, "such harmless fools as a body can come across along a river, I tell you."

A river, I thought to myself.

Then we talked of railroading, for I brought it up. I thought he'd like the notion of them men racing the big engines along certain stretches of track.

He heartily agreed. "The upper brass regularly turns a blind eye to the practice, Miss Clara. I hear the leg between Montgomery and Muncy's a local favorite."

"That's the one I had in mind," I told him, and wishing to seem knowledgeable, I added, "The Reading Engines always beat the Penncy Atlantics."

"They're ten-wheelers, Miss Clara. Quicker at the start at all, ma'am." He fixed his hat, looked off toward the mountain, then went on with, "Give them big ole Penncy Atlantics some rollin' space, and a body'll see a right pretty sight."

Then he reminded the left rear mare to get back to work with a quick, light lash, and said to me, "That river of yours, your Susquehanna beyond the trees and the fields, she's a pretty one, and large with lumberin', but she'll be forgotten. The times comin', Miss Clara, are for the worshippers of the machine."

Then we both went quiet, and I don't know how it come about, but our talk then slowly worked toward the natures of caring and affection, as our faces stayed upon the rutted, wet road before us. For we shied up, we did, but we stayed to it, considering our shyness of the subject, and it was a most special sharing of ideas for two common souls such as us back then.

Between the two of us, we fished mostly about two main things. The first was broken hearts, and the strength and the lastingness of that deep pain. I think this talk warmed us considerable for as we stared ahead, Mr. Finley's left arm lightly grazed mine several times, and I didn't withdraw as he told me, "It's somehow sadder for those who never had to live through it, Miss Clara. They're missin' a right powerful, lonesome journey."

Our second topic was love's struggles, and I mainly listened, save for, "I know little of it, Mr. Finley, save for my Emma, and that's of course a different thing and all."

"Well, Miss Clara," he said as he smiled to the road ahead, "I'll wager you I know even less."

"Well then," I braved up, with a smile of my own, "I now prod you, sir, for what you do know."

He figured there were mainly two struggles, but then he tamed his talk and went less hard, calling them "hungerings," before quieting altogether as a big coach gained on us from behind, passing our load of hay, on their own way to the city. I took notice of four well-dressed passengers behind their coachman, but I didn't know them. Perhaps from Muncy or beyond, I guessed, as Mr. Finley then spoke softly.

"Miss Waltz, it's 'bout faithfulness, love is, is all I know."

I purposely brushed his left arm with my right arm, aiming at adjusting my bonnet. "What else do you know?" I looked straight ahead. "I'd truly care to know, Mr. Finley."

"It's a bargain that strikes itself in two people, so in two ways, and both try to meet up between one another, which is right dif'cult enough, but then they gots to stay met up and all, all nice and all.

He turned his smile away from me, as though regretful for having said what he said. And then we both forced a look to one another, which turned to quiet smiles that came easy, as our faces rocked with the wagon's ride.

"Plum foolish of me, Miss Waltz, to ramble so."

"Plum foolish of you not to, sir, if you think of such things," I said back to him, as I looked forward again.

"Well, Miss Clara, I do thank you, for a body needs someone to talk to from time to far time."

* * *

At Mrs. Snyder's I thought of Mr. Finley a good deal, and I even related some of those ponderings to old Mrs. Snyder herself as I fed her. But I only called him my friend and such, for I never truly knew what was going on within her stillness. To be quicker with this, I very much looked forward to my return to Montoursville upon the wagon with him, and hoped so for fine weather for the ride.

And three days later he did come for me, after another of Mrs. Snyder's daughters-in-law showed up to relieve me, and such a ride it'd come to be.

And we were both content with this, as far as I could see, for we smiled true to one another upon his arrival. To spark up talk, once moving, I pointed out several of the circus bills that had sprung up around the city, on fences and telegraph poles, on the side of one passing trolley and on bigger trees, all tacked up in days, for the circus was to arrive in a month and a week. Middle of June.

And, indeed, the big show did start us talking, of the big top and of the brass bands that all in the show moved to. "I like the spectacle of the opening day parade," I told him. "I wish I could have Emma up here in the city for the arrival of their train."

Mr. Finley liked the animals, especially the camels and the elephants from across the seas. I, the silly monkeys in their colorful baby clothes, at the ends of collars and leashes, and both of us, the lions in their cages.

"The fliers, Miss Clara, is my favorite act, though," he told me.

It took me a moment. "The trapeze people, you mean?" I smiled at him.

"Yes, like fairies come to flesh, 'specially if you're sittin' far off and can't hear 'em breathin'."

I was also glad we were talking so, for it pushed down other thoughts, thoughts of Charlie Logan, who would have been traveling with this same circus show. Then up ahead of us, up in Market Square, we both saw a gathering commotion.

As our own big team worked along with the eastbound traffic of Third Street, we could see it was youngsters and grown-ups alike, with a couple of dogs even, surrounding a decorated platform. It was a sent-ahead circus act, you see, one of several to come, to whet folks' appetites for the big show itself.

"Would you like to stop, Mr. Finley? Only for a few minutes?" I asked him.

"It might be right fun, mighten' it, Miss Clara?"

"Oh yes, I do think so. Then we'll get right along."

"Just momentarily. We gots dung to load up in Faxon." He eyed the goings-on up on the platform. He had a near boyish look to him, in spite of his whiskers. It was in his eyes, you see.

I waited for Mr. Finley as he tied the team fast, then we milled into the crowd together. Beneath their colorful banner, there was a snake charmer performing at the time. Two midgets worked the crowd, trailed by laughing youngsters, as did a fortune sayer, draped in silks and jewels. I wanted none of her, detestable I recalled from James or Deuteronomy. Then hollers and screams went up, and all turned to that part of the crowd.

"The world's only tongueless woman!" proudly proclaimed a pointing ringmaster from the platform, as he appeared to excuse the snake charmer.

From the side of their platform, the woman parted our crowd with her wide-opened, dark mouth, as the kids, the midgets and the dogs kicked up dust behind us.

Then the platform master sang out again. "Fire eaters! Coming up! Three at a time! But first, ladies and gentlemen of this fine city of lumbering, allow me to most graciously and most humbly present to you, none other than the real, in his own flesh and blood, the grown-up man of Huckleberry Finn!! And his most faithful, most true companion, the Nigger Jim!!"

My own heart leapt, it did. And I stole a look to Mr. Finley, beside me, but that boyishness was already gone. And his old Adam's apple stroked hard, two times.

Two men climbed the platform from behind, and the second was indeed an old colored man, looked near crippled, dressed in rags. The old white man's clothes weren't much tidier, and his hair was long and silvery as he removed his big straw hat and bowed to the murmuring crowd.

Hank Finley, silent beside me, watched on.

The Huckleberry Finn man went first, strutting to and fro across their platform, talking and boasting of where all he'd been and of what all he'd done and seen. To questions he welcomed from the crowd, he was most down on and critical of Tom Sawyer, whom he said, ". . . gained hisself a wife, a home with kids! Why, he went and gone civilized on me!"

He knelt and patted some children on their heads, inviting them to touch of the old Negro man's head with, "Come young'ins, have a good feel of Jim's wool." And many did, for we seldom saw colored folks about our parts. Then a man from our crowd asked him if he knew Mr. Samuel Clemons.

" 'A course I knowed him! Glory be, I made 'im rich!" he laughed, as did many. "Why, a man couldn't make up from his own head the story I lived, young feller."

Then he strutted some more, behind the colored man, and his silver locks waved as he told the crowd of his panning for gold somewhere out west. Then that one question came. From an older man behind us, loud and determined.

"What of the murdered boy? What of him out there along the Ohio River?"

I tried to look to Mr. Finley, beside me, but couldn't fully, but I saw his chest swell fast, in a heaving inhale.

The Huckleberry Finn man replied, "I done heared 'em all! Every cowpie story out there. What I'd barter off to come upon the coward that begun this one, I tell you. Then, I tell you all, every one of you, I'll kill a man down, I will!"

Then he settled himself, like he had good practice at it, speaking softly, yet loud for the crowd. "I have kilt, I have. Savages. Sioux and Chennye along with Major Reno." Then he slowed, nice and steady with it. "And I would'a kilt hellish more if'in we could'a made it to Custer's flank as it were planned, by Lord in Heaven!"

Well, he went on some, he did, and the old Negro, he stood to come down and move about our crowd, but I listened no more. I was near ashamed of myself for trying as hard as I was at noticing the swelling of Mr. Finley's eyes as he stood silent beside me.

I didn't look again as I asked him, "Shall we go, Mr. Finley?"

He only nodded in agreement. I touched him, and turned him, and we made our way back to the team.

* * *

I said no more as he worked our wagon into the streets of the east end for the dung. Nor would I talk as it was loaded, for I knew not what to say. Oh how I wished that day that I could trade my secret for his, but he had two for my one, you see. Who he was, and why on earth did he do what he did?

But once moving out through the quiet farmlands, between Faxon's east end and the big Sand Hill curve in the road, I could hold my tongue no more.

"Do you suppose that was truly them?"

"No, ma'am. Just circus folks is all."

"But it could have been."

"The famous Nigger Jim's long dead. Runned over by a train, Miss Clara." He paused, then added, "Like the whole beautiful land, I tell ya."

"How do you know?" I braved up, staring ahead.

"Oh, a man I was once acquainted with. He told me, and he weren't given to untruths, Miss Clara."

"Well, how about that Huckleberry Finn man? He sounded so real and so sure. Some in the crowd figured it to be him, I'm sure."

"Oh, Miss Clara," he said as he rewrapped the reins, "who knows, but that weren't him."

The left rear mare acted up again. We both looked to her.

"What sort of a man do you suppose a boy such as him in that storybook would have grown up to become?"

He lashed the mare fast and hard, correcting her. I flinched.

"I don't know, but a lot of folks likes speculatin'."

Then we both paused our conversation for a stretch, as the clopping of our team and our warm load passed a carriage tied to a tree off the road. Sweethearts, I thought.

"Perhaps such as that John Chapman fella was," he continued, without my asking. "Ya know, Miss Clara? The apple tree plantin' fella?"

I nodded, and replied, "Just roaming you mean, Mr. Finley?"

"Yes, 'cepting not vain. Famous in a folk-talk sorta way, 'cepting not vain about it, Miss Clara."

Then he breathed deep. "Preachy to none, Miss Clara. No Bible, and forgive me for that, for I know your tenderness for the Good Book. And no trail of trees, neither. Just wishin' to tend to his own affairs is all."

Then he quieted, and looked off long south, at the rising of our Bald Eagle Ridge. I looked to the team. A fresh line of blood glistened red on the working right-side rump of the quieted mare.

I forgave him for that. And then I left him alone with the other, for I'll never forget seeing, from the corner of my eye, his one bony hand leave his gathered reins, rising to wipe at his looking-away eyes.

CHAPTER 9

I left him alone with it for a good part of that May. You see, I only wanted things to be better, things having anything to do with either of the killings, and more and more, things between he and I, about our separate duties and responsibilities to the Deacons and about their farm.

But I thought of him, I did. I didn't leave him alone in my prayers, nor in my thoughts. It was near spiritual for me, to watch him from sometimes near and from sometimes afar, but especially from afar. I liked the dawn the best, in the misty distance. That man risen, from the boy. That boy. That ghost to all others, but real, and handsome, like a gift to only me. The aging of Huckleberry Finn, in from the wilderness of thirty years, I figured. In, for I knew of his secret, and I imagined, in again, whenever someone, anyone, caught on to his true being.

I wished to promise him that his secret was safe with me. I thought of him long and hard, and I thought of his boyhood friend, Tom Sawyer, and I thought of that Mr. Samuel Clemons man, the knowing god of one of the two, for I recalled back then seeing a photograph, in the *Gazette*, or more probably, in one of the Deacons' *Harper's* or *Atlantic Monthly* magazines, of that Mr. Samuel Clemons, all in his white hair and white suit, smoking his pipe alongside the grown man of Tom Sawyer, he too dressed fine and looking regular serious about his work with the congress. And I thought of Mr. Hank Finley, of how that Mark Twain man was also the unknowing god to him, a man toiling in other work, in his silence about himself, about the very farm that took myself in so long before. Then I thought over the two of us, two souls shaped by the hands and deeds of others.

And another fortnight worked by as I lived with my knowledge of him being so near. A stay with Mrs. Snyder came up, and Rebecca, who I relieved early due to her advanced condition, had kinder words for her aged mother-in-law, but I thought so only because I wasn't due for my own caring for another two days. But about my stay that time, it was Mrs. Snyder's nice big house, and if its walls could talk, that I pondered, beside her in her silence. But she'd tell me, she would, in other ways as I sat with her after having dressed her for bed. She'd tell me through packed-away photographs of her house, with the trees and the backgrounds and the people I knew all looking so much younger. I wondered when she and her husband bought the house, and how they managed that, and then I felt a touch sad with no house, nor any hope of one of my own, only mine and Emma's room within the home of the Deacons. I'd cheer up though, in a few days, for it was Hank Finley who'd retrieve me while receiving iron strappings and other such heavy hardware from a Williamsport foundry, for a new outbuilding going up.

And as we talked on our ride home, I grew silly and simple, you see, and quiet too, pretending that Mr. Finley and I were husband and wife, for we could have looked it to the city people along the streets. Mr. Finley, aged with labor, yet handsome and solemn. And myself his wife, true and just. Of course we could have also been taken as father and daughter, but I pushed those notions away, in favor of the ones that took me away from real concerns. I pushed them away, desiring instead to look settled and married, about the duties of my husband beside me as we tended to our lives.

* * *

Oh, how I wished things to be better, and how they did seem to be working so, until two days after, when more visitors came to the Deacons' big house.

It was during one of those spells when Mr. Deacon could have used some fitting company, for he was again after Elizabeth to pay him mind over concerns of his own that she just didn't have any banter for. It was also after dinner, for I was cleaning up as Mr. Deacon was going on about the people of America as, "Thirty-five million strong, Elizabeth. Up from the paltry three or four million of the revolution. We're sitting to be world leaders come the turn of the century."

Then it was work reform, I believe, as he smoked while Elizabeth and Sarah and Joshua took their dessert. He brought up our own valley's Saw Dust Wars of the 1870's, when I was just a schoolgirl. Even I could recall the big strikes, for the State Militia was called in. "Soon folks'll be fixing to strike over their twelve-hour work days, my dear, not happy with the gains they've earned." He puffed away as we heard horses approach the house.

We thought nothing of it, not even as the men's boots sounded out upon the planks of the verandah, not even as I told Elizabeth, "I'll see to the door, Mrs. Deacon." Not until I swung the big door open to none other than Joseph Logan and Stacy Kremer themselves.

I stood still, dumbfounded.

"Who is it, Clara?" Elizabeth called from the dining room.

"Visitors, Mrs. Deacon," I stumbled. Then I looked away, or down. "Mr. Deacon," I managed. "Two men, sir, to speak with you."

"We've come to have a word with you, Miss Clara Waltz, with Mr. Deacon's permission of course," began Joseph, looking so much older to me, handsome but older, perhaps tired from the killing, I figured later.

Stacy Kremer just stood there, stiff and scared looking, nearly as scared as myself, as Henry Deacon came to the foyer, studying our guests.

"Excuse the children, Elizabeth, dear," he said without looking at her. "Come in, gentlemen. My name's Henry Deacon," he stated without offering his hand, waving them into the parlor.

I smelled liquor, and hoped that Mr. Deacon smelled it as well.

Then Stacy Kremer spoke his first. "We've been acquainted, sir, through Grange work. Perhaps you don't recall." His voice shook, and his eyes darted to me, then about the room.

"Please be seated, gentlemen. May Clara get you anything?" Mr. Deacon asked calm, and most deliberate.

"Just the truth, Mr. Deacon," Joseph answered fast, turning to glare at me.

"This woman has already sat for proper questioning, as the law saw necessary. Two times, if it were any of your affair, and of which it isn't," Mr. Deacon spoke for me.

Stacy Kremer trembled and made a sound, but I couldn't tell what. Joseph's face flared, all eyes and nostrils.

"I'll tell you, sir! And that whore too!" he leveled hard as his voice rose, "of what is my affair. My own brother murdered, sir. Like a dog! By a savage, on my own front porch, not but walls away from my sleeping wife and children!"

Mr. Deacon recoiled, and I felt for him, for this new misery.

"I know nothing of it, Mr. Logan," I cut in. "And I've answered so many questions, I truly have. And I truly don't know who killed your brother. I truly don't."

"You're a liar, Clara Waltz!" burst in Stacy Kremer, with his balding thin hair all wild, with one hand rising to work it down. "Oh, you—you—you evil bitch dog you, after all I offered you," he added as his voice fell off and shook so that I thought he might cry.

"Gentlemen," Henry Deacon collected himself, "I believe you've been drinking and—"

"Our supper matters none, sir," Joseph cut in, breathing hard. I shot a look to the window, seeing Sarah and my own Emma, through the lacy curtains, running out toward the bottoms where the help put up.

"I believe this visitation is over, gentlemen," Mr. Deacon's own voice hardened.

Then Joseph turned to me. "What matters here is two men dead. Too awful queer to be coincidence, Clara Waltz."

I could smell the liquor stronger then, as he talked right at me, even over Mr. Deacon's sweet pipe tobacco.

Then Joseph continued, "I swear if this all comes to be from the doings of a whore such as yourself, I'll see you hanged dead in the gallows with my own eyes. I swear to God I will."

"Not in my house, Mr. Logan!" Mr. Deacon rose into standing.

"And what about mine?" Joseph asked to him, angry and sad.

And the two of them said more, but it must have been softening, for I can't recall it now for my own thinking of the two girls running off so, which saddened me and shamed me. Both, you see, were in Sarah's dresses. Only one was new, from the catalog, and the other, of course, was not.

Then there were heavy footsteps coming up through the back, then in through the kitchen. Stacy Kremer's eyes flashed that way, then back to us. Joe Logan looked to me, then toward the kitchen way as Mr. Finley came into the room with another of the farmhands. Little George, most called him. But it was Hank Finley who spoke.

"Forgive our bustin' in, Mr. Deacon." He breathed heavy from his hurrying. Then he removed that tattered, big brimmed hat. "The fencing, sir, out to the backside of the lower Mill Stream pasture," he paused, and I saw the lump slide in his throat, "is that the line you wish us to be tending to?"

"Perhaps, Hank, you and George could see these gentlemen to their way home, or elsewhere," Mr. Deacon replied, smoking heavily at his pipe.

"You don't care, Clara Waltz," Joseph said to this, "about all the others hurt. Loved ones, family. Why, my own mother doesn't speak but a sobbing here or there—"

"Come, sirs," Mr. Finley spoke humbly, nodding toward the archway into the foyer.

"You're evil, you are. You'll get worse than you ever—"

"Now, sirs, it'd be most wise, I'm sure," continued Mr. Finley, raising, and holding his hat between my face and Joseph Logan's, as though protecting me.

"I know you. I remember you," blurted out Stacy Kremer. "You was with her, you was. Up in the city that day."

"In the service of Mr. Deacon, sir. And in his service as we speak, I ask you kindly to leave this home and farm."

"Or what?" Joseph demanded to all three.

"Or Little George here goes and fetches Mr. Reese, our constable, sir. As I stays here," Hank Finley replied evenly, keeping his aging eyes fast to Joseph's. They stared at one another only briefly, before all four filed out the front door.

Mr. Deacon said nothing to me as he stepped from his parlor, and I wished that he would have, for I felt most alone as I heard the horses ride off.

But mind you, for a first I didn't fear. And I felt a warm closeness to that Mr. Finley, an evil thing that I'd pray over, again and again. Oh me oh my, how I also then prayed over how my own past must have looked to, or been told to Mr. Finley. Yes, I wondered over that too back then, as our two lonesome paths seemed to be growing closer, toward a keeping of company.

But no more did I fear, for it was Horace Will's very own killer who led them away, and none knew it save he and myself.

* * *

But things that spring stayed dark for me, in spite of the birds all being back, and in spite of the leaves of the trees flushing out green, or how my laundry dried fresh and clean so fast out on the lines. You see, I received another letter, and unbeknownst to Elizabeth, for I got to it first, being sent up into town for the mail. And I was glad of this too, for I didn't need her knowing it. Not that letter, anyway, and not then, for more darkness was to come.

The letter was unsigned, and spiteful and mean, calling me names and warning me of things its writer was only nasty about, and not particular over. I saved it, hiding it amongst my things as I set a mind to get more from Hank Finley. I didn't rightly know more of what, but I was taking an aim, you see, and I prayed over it, too, to have some help with it.

My first chance came one evening after dinner, just days later. It was still mid-May, with the big garden set to seed, you see, which of course came second to the fields. Anyway, Emma learned that Mr. Finley intended to fish for spring catties down below the federal dam on the Loyalsock, and she managed to get young Joshua Deacon excited over it too. Sarah dismissed the notion, for the Rakestraw twins were over, both cute as buttons and silly as anything. As for myself, I assured Elizabeth that I'd watch over Joshua and Emma, who fetched two poles and a couple of throw lines from the yard shed.

Well, the logs were light behind the dam, and there weren't many others about either, only some bigger children, downstream from the hole where Mr. Finley decided we should lay out our own lines. In time, the youngsters downstream had themselves a fire going, which of course gained the interest of Emma and Joshua so I let them go, being that one of the children was a Reese relative, and being that Emma and Joshua stayed within eyeshot of me and Mr. Finley.

And then Mr. Finley and I talked some, and it was our usual about the Deacon farm subjects, for I suppose that made us both comfortable, a place to start, you see, as our talks always seemed to take root. Then I thought of a story for him, one that I liked in particular, and had yet to share with him.

"Mr. Finley, you ever hear of the tale of Esther MacDowell?" I asked him.

"No, I have not, Miss Clara. What can you tell me of her?"

"Well, she was a spooky sort of creature. At least according to her tale, from the upper part of our valley, earlier this century. You know of the town of Jersey Shore?"

"Not a'tall, Clara," Hank answered me as he watched the Loyalsock. "Excepting that she lies bout midway upriver, between Williamsport and Lock Haven."

I sat down on a flat rock and smoothed my apron upon my lap, and checked quick to the children. "Well, Mr. Finley, she was about as near an evil creature as one can be, and yet still be liked somehow."

Mr. Finley lobbed out another throw line. It plunked. "Tell me of her, Miss Clara." He smiled. "I'd like to hear this one."

"Well, it was about 1810 or 1820," I went on, "back when Jersey Shore was nothing more than a street of a dozen or so cabins."

Hank Finley listened keenly.

"And this young Esther, she appeared, or turned up, unknown, one early morning, found gagged at her mouth and bound naked to a tree before the cabin of a man named Martin Reese."

I shied up a bit over the naked part, but I pushed on. "This Martin Reese, he of course freed her, and covered her and took her to his reverend's home, whose family took her in properly, for the forlorn thing that she was. All were shocked of course."

Her tale was as tragic as could be, and Hank listened well, never interrupting me as he strung up a second cattie and tossed back a small carp. So I went on.

"This young Esther MacDowell, she told the men, back then, of her wealthy family back in Montreal, sending her off to family, south, in far off Kentucky, and of the trusted guide who was employed to see her through her long journey, across near all wilderness."

"I'm listening, Miss Clara," Hank told me.

"Well, greed and lust must have took the man." I shied again. "For he could take no more and he robbed her and worse, and then he left her for dead one dark night, in the trees, tied to one of them, across from Jersey Shore's big island, never seeing Martin Reese's unlit cabin."

Mr. Finley looked toward the youngsters downstream, then nodded to myself to continue.

"Well, a manhunt, of course, took place, of a grand and angry size, all the way up and down our Bald Eagle Ridge, and on the south side too."

"Any luck?"

"None, for no villain was found. He must have slipped away into the heavy forests, the men figured back then. And, oh my, how the sympathy and the gifts of clothes and jewelry began pouring in toward Jersey Shore, for the preacher's house, as word of Esther's abuse spread along our stretch of the Susquehanna. She rightly became an attraction," I told Mr. Finley as he fished beside me.

"I'll bet she did, Miss Clara."

"But it wouldn't last. Not more than a month as the story goes."

Hank looked down to me. "That so." He smiled. "What become of her?"

"Well, this man journeyed upriver from down in Milton, to speculate on a track of land. He, of course, come to hear of her then, like the others, and he wished to deliver his own sympathies with a visit."

To this Mr. Finley grinned wider, watching the stream.

"Well, Esther grew terrible shy before him, and the Milton man knew why right off, for this girl had worked for him only the year before, disguised as a boy, laboring as a journeyman tailor."

"Go on, Miss Waltz," smiled Mr. Finley, wrapping wet line.

"Well, he called her to task for it, and he charged her with robbing his own shop as well, and all this before the stricken eyes of the preacher, his family and neighbors."

Then I smiled too, for making him smile, before going on with, "Esther then wept for forgiveness, which was of course granted by one and all. She was a lost thing, a young lamb, alone in the world, she pleaded. And then she took flight herself, Mr. Finley, that very night, managing to tote off all of her gifts, after robbing the good preacher to boot."

Mr. Finley laughed aloud to that part, in fact twice, which pleased me of course, for I too liked that story, and in some way, that bad, awful girl. I thought then, and still think now, that it was her loneliness that made her a bit like me. Oh, she was sinister she was, but I felt for her just the same. We were sisters, she and I, to my thinking, one good and the other bad, yet both alone, save ourselves, sisters in loneliness.

"Folks tend to figure two ways about that story, Mr. Finley," I said to him as he stood upon the rocks of the edge of the Loyalsock.

"How so, Miss Clara?"

"Well, either that she was an evil one, and a thief, or that the hole darned scheme was, well, a bit funny."

He smiled broad, fixing fresh bait to another hook.

"Parading herself as a boy was no crime, Miss Clara. No crime a'tall," he laughed lightly. "But stealin' was, of course. But a body'd have to know more of her to judge. There's more to her tale, you see."

Then he cast that same hook out to a plop in the slow passing water, and said with his back still to me, "No, Miss Clara, I don't care to judge folks. There's plenty enough of that goin' around."

Then I surprised my own self, but apparently not Mr. Finley beside me with, "Would you care to judge me?"

He turned to me then, and he looked so kind and true.

"No, Miss Clara. No, I wouldn't, because I don't have enough of that tale neither, nor have I ever ast for it."

Oh, how I wanted to trade his secret for mine, so I gathered up my breath and went ahead with it.

"We've come to be friends, haven't we, Mr. Finley?"

"Yes, to my great pleasure I like to believe that, Miss Waltz," he said softer, sitting down beside me. A couple of loose rocks shifted.

I looked straight ahead, across the creek and into the trees. "I fear so, that you've heard things of me. Of my past, and perhaps of my character. Of my situation, you see."

"People talk, Miss Clara, oh they do."

"Would you care for the truth, Mr. Finley?" I asked him, still looking into those trees.

"Only if ya need to tell it, Miss Waltz," he answered me, looking into the same trees, adjusting his hat that he wore out upon that ice, what seemed so long before.

So I told him all of it, right there, us sitting together on that stony bank of the Loyalsock. I told him of my youth, and of my fancy for a much-younger-at-the-time Joseph Logan. I told him of my father, and of the other four men, naming all of them, taking note that Mr. Finley never so much as flinched to the name of Horace Wills.

I told him of that swinging lantern, and of how they were so rough with me. And of my torn-off clothes, and of my shame back then. And I told him of how folks thought me a liar and a whore, and of how time, and Pastor English, had delivered me and my infant Emma to the Deacons, where I've remained most gratefully, and with fidelity.

"And here ever since, and up until I found you?" He looked to me.

"Yes." And I added slowly, "And now it's come to be, Mr. Finley, that I'm somehow figured to be a either a killer myself, or in with one," to which he again never so much as batted either of his nice old eyes.

Then we talked of what evil would drive men to do such crimes. I figured the Devil, and said so.

He reminded me again, "I know little of Scripture, Miss Waltz, so I really can't fit it."

Instead, he talked of those crimes, that the two of us tiptoed about, as punishments, and he struggled some too.

"Punishments gone wild and hungering, Miss Clara, and turned into terrible wishes come true."

Then he stood and straightened and breathed deep, working at wrapping in his throw lines as the children were returning to us. Then he told me, without looking at me, "I do figure that somehow that Mr. Wills, and that Logan feller too, may have mostly gotten their just rewards, Miss Clara. Sometimes it just works that way."

Which led us to fairness, as we and Emma and Joshua then made our way home. Joshua mostly played about, and mostly with Emma, as Mr. Finley and I talked, mostly in a guarded way, for Emma's sake, or maybe for our own.

"As for fairness," I told him as we walked, "the Lord will dole it out at Judgment," as I smoothed at my soiled apron.

"I believe it's man's place, here and now," Mr. Finley was quick. "But maybe near impossible, Miss Clara, for most men are broken," and he troubled with that one. "Broken, I do believe, even those men doing the evening-outs of other's rights and wrongs."

And in no time we were back, parting company upon the thick grass of the Deacons' wide yard. He handed me his line of five nice fat bullheads. One gave a quick shake, still alive. I took the fish. Then, "Mr. Finley," I breathed, "will you ever tell me the story of yourself?"

"Oh, Miss Clara, Miss Clara Waltz," he declared straight to my eyes. Then his voice softened, to a near whisper. "That tale has never brought good to me."

"I'll never tell, Mr. Finley," I whispered back. "Not ever."

And I kept it to his eyes too, before minding myself, flustering to be so familiar with him out there in the big yard where any could see us.

He looked a little sad as he removed that tattered hat of his. Then he pulled back his long silver hair, and he looked right at me. "Miss Clara," he said as he smiled a touch, "someday I just might give it one more try."

* * *

And I can recall that night as well, for Emma's sudden ponderings, at least sudden for me.

It was well after all went quiet and dark in the big Deacon house. The crickets were alive outside, and the air was cool and moving at our curtains. Our prayers were said and our lamp was snuffed for the night, when sometime after I figured Emma to be asleep, her little voice asked me, "Mama, why don't I have a father?"

"Oh me oh my, Emma," I whispered. "We'll talk of that, I promise. What ever made you think of such a thing?"

"I don't know, Mama. You always said Jesus put us here special, and watches us so, with the angels. I was just wondering."

"Emma, Emma, dear thing, don't fret so," I whispered and pulled her closer to me. "Sleep now. Sleep."

You see, I didn't yet have it figured what I'd someday tell her. I worked on it from time to time, but the furthest I ever got was that I would not tell her falsehoods—no dead husband or such.

But I just didn't have it figured. I only knew that I wished to wait until she was of understanding, of a womanly way with her age. And I was thinking of that when she spoke again, softly.

"Mama, don't you think Mr. Finley would make a good father for us?"

I liked the "us", I did. And I worried over how much of mine and Hank Finley's talking she could have taken to upon our walk home over the paths.

"He'd make a fine father, Emma, for anyone. He's a good man. Now go to sleep, honey. Sleep," I told her.

But I did like the "us" as she quieted for good, as I looked out into the starry darkness that pushed lightly into our little room.

I could rest, so I did. For I didn't know that nice night of how my days would darken once again. And, oh me oh my, how soon.

* * *

The next few days passed and I did see some of Mr. Finley, but I asked him none of the story of himself. I'd bide my time, I would, in favor of other talk, for he was such a nice man to converse with.

Amongst several run-ins with him, I shared more of my recent affection for Mrs. Snyder, who I was to stay with the coming week. I was moving freezer box scraps, and leftovers from the big house out to the help's quarters. Another time, as one of the Paulhamus brothers was on the property, scraping and shaving and shoeing horses, Mr. Finley and I talked of his other thoughts. I recall the story of "Alter Rock" as his take called it.

I knew of several of the tales, for each was a little different, even in naming the rock itself. "Some call it 'Steeple Rock,' " I told Mr. Finley. "Some 'Chimney Rock,' and others 'Pulpit Rock.' I've never seen it myself, Mr. Finley, nor am I certain as to where it's located, save somewhere along the Susquehanna's north branch, in the forests north of Scranton and Wilkes-Barre. Coal country, I believe."

"Have you heard the tale of the young savage called Two Pines, Miss Clara?" Mr. Finley asked me.

"He killed someone is all I know."

"Yes, might'a been a French trapper, but for different reasons with each of the tellings of his tale, I understand." Mr. Finley smiled.

And then we shared those tellings, leastways the ones we knew of. And each one had him climbing that rock-thing, jutting up and out from the river, but from there they changed. One had him killing himself, another had him killed by other trappers and a third had him vanishing all spooky in a fast fog. Each story, though, ended with two lonesome-looking pine trees growing atop that tall rock.

"I like that tale, Miss Clara, told to me by some feller down at the Catawissa Line, then corrected to me by Little George," he said, smiling, "with Little George's take on it."

"Well, I'm happy for you then." I smiled back.

"Well, thank you, Miss Clara, but I must confess that I don't take a whole lot of stock in a tale with too many sides. Nonetheless, I'd sure like to see that rock one day. Must be a pretty sight, rising tall and solid and still, up and out of the slow passing of that other Susquehanna."

Odd enough too, for in that brief spell I also took notice to Mr. Twain's *The Adventures of Tom Sawyer* amongst Mr. Deacon's books as I dusted one afternoon, and thought of reading it, or better still, the one about Huckleberry Finn, if I could come across a copy. But the notion passed, it did, as I recalled hearing one time or another, probably while tending to a dinner, that it was a most difficult book to read, especially whenever the colored man, Jim, talked. So I just thought of it, I suppose, while attending to my duties. I mostly knew the story anyway, for it was quite famous of course, and the story, you see, didn't interest me as much as how the one boy come up, in real life, to become rich and famous, as the other couldn't, or wouldn't, even take a claim to his own name.

Then, out of nowhere, the *Gazette* ran more on the killings. The two stories were printed side by side on the opinion page, and Joseph Logan was quoted in both. Both stories read like he and the reporters were together in fed-upness. Both also circled around a nameless woman, a dangerous, evil creature who held the key to the valley's fear, yet refused to cooperate. Justice would be served though, guaranteed, and both apologized for not naming the woman, due to hindering the law's ongoing efforts.

I thought no one else noticed the stories, until Mr. Deacon himself approached me on the back porch the following afternoon, with that same *Gazette* in hand, telling me, "These are hard times, Clara. Be faithful." I watched for more, but none came.

Then the Deacon house livened, for Mr. Deacon, quite in the quiet, went ahead and ordered one of those portable indoor bathing tubs, with a safety brand coal burning water heater. Even Elizabeth hadn't known of it until several of the hands, Mr. Finley included, brought it up from the Catawissa Depot in three large crates.

Oh, there was a jolly good time over it too, from the unloading of the crates from the wagon, to all the sawing and banging away as the farmhands fit it into the big back workroom off the kitchen. Mr. Deacon's aim, I gathered, was to wall off a section of that room, for his privacy of course.

And that work was still shaping along when things darkened once more by that week's end.

* * *

They darkened about another of the Deacon's fine dinner parties, another that started mid-afternoon one Saturday, to go on into that early evening. The good Reverend Ashhurst was there, as was Samuel and Ellen Wills. Two other couples, who I knew little of, attended as well. I can't recall the names of the Williamsport banker and his wife, but the logging man was Mr. John Barclay, along with his wife, Mary. They had been around before, you see. I liked his wife. She was very courteous to me, and dark eyed and dark haired and spooky pretty. Only big Amos Reese and his wife were delayed, said to arrive by dinner, their daughter reported.

In their leisure there was, of course, bicycling and croquet and phonograph listening. And as I, myself, attended to preparing their big dinner, Emma and Sarah tended to their lighter refreshments, sharing the toting about of the baby. Little ladies they were fast becoming.

In time, all took places about the big table, amidst laughter over the games they played, then more over the banker's dogs, of which he was so proud. I can't recall his name, mind you, but I can the subject of his dogs.

Then all quieted to the softer clatter of their dining, and, as usual, to the men's larger concerns. One subject, agreeable to the men, concerned the congress and protective tariffs, of which I knew nothing.

The banker wished to debate another, of which he said, "Millions of dollars of surplus, earmarked as pensions for the still-living Civil War veterans. Northern only of course."

"And most are still alive, having served as mere children," Mr. Deacon worried, "yet in their thirties and forties, such as ourselves."

"But deserving, nonetheless," cut in Mr. Barclay, as all quieted, for he had a G.A.R. command of his own when just a boy himself.

Before the serving of dessert, their talk lightened to that of President Harrison's pushing the notion of rural free delivery of the mail. I recall this because this was when Amos Reese wrapped lightly upon the Deacon front door.

His wife was with him, and I found it disturbing how she stole a fast look to me as I took her wraps, before she greeted the other wives rather quietly.

I suppose there was little need for privacy anymore, so big Amos took none. "Forgive me, Henry. I was detained by the Williamsport constables in my own office."

The thought of his big kind self being kept to that chair fleeted through my mind, but not for long, as he announced to all about the Deacon table, "Mr. Joseph Logan was discovered near beaten to death, sometime last night. Just two blocks from his own home up in Newberry."

A good stirring arose about the table, of which I only heard pieces of on account of my own being taken aback.

"Will he survive?" asked the banker's wife.

"Our very own Jack The Ripper," leveled that Mr. Barclay, in that deep voice of his.

Then I was touched from behind, upon both my shoulders. And it was Elizabeth Deacon, joined by Emma, from the parlor, where the baby was. Emma was indeed learning, I gathered, as Reverend Ashhurst and the banker went on about that Ripper person.

"Ours is just a killer," the reverend answered him. "After something certain, not just anyone."

"It's been over two years now, for them English, Reverend, and still no monster brought to justice," the banker spoke soft.

"But theirs is a beast, sir. One of hysterical, evil dimensions, tearing apart his victims."

"We're at a dinner table, gentlemen," Mr. Deacon reminded the men of their debate.

" Ours, sir," the reverend softened, "is something different. Evil, indeed, yet different."

Oh me oh my, it's dark to me now for it was dark to me then. But my recollection of it now also takes me to that night, and how Mrs. Deacon had earlier tried to help me clean up from that big dinner, and of how I tried to tell her that I needed the busyness, I did.

And then after the Deacon house was dark and quiet, as I laid with Emma, with she either awake or asleep, for I didn't check, I again recalled another terror from that night of so long before, as I had with each new misery. I recalled boasting amidst their laughter, amidst my own dear struggle. It was harelipped Horace Wills, claiming that as a boy his own father couldn't dare leave him alone with the colts. He was at his second helping of me, you see. And as I laid with my Emma that night, I felt most evil for feeling content that he was the first to stand, and the first to fall to Righteousness' calling.

And then I prayed for myself, and then some over him, asking the Lord if Mr. Finley was evil trying to do goodness, or if he was goodness trying to do evil. Then a verse came to me, and stayed with me for some time. I believed the first line to be: "You have taken of plenty upon the Earth and have gone in for sensual pleasure." The next, though, came to me most clear. "You have fattened your hearts on the day of the slaughter."

Before I slept myself, I thought again of Mr. Hank Finley, and I thought of how I was going to ask him who he really was. And I looked out our little window with that thought that night. Light clouds wisped across the lonely moon. Then I thought, too, of how I was going to tell him, save me, exactly what I did see with my own eyes from within that fallen tree that icy early morning.

CHAPTER 10

As it came to be, I again left him alone with his secrets—one, who he was, another that I knew to be sure of, and, of course, the two more that I feared. I left him alone on into that time of the prettiest of mid-May. Due to Joe Logan's recent beating, and due to my own growing happiness over mine and Mr. Finley's friendship at the time, I decided to bide my time, just a bit longer.

You see, that darkness lifted some, or perhaps turned to something else, a dream-like time for me as I came to learn, through listening as best I could, that at least Joe Logan was still alive. Talk about the big house and farm had it that way, then the *Gazette*, too, carried word of his well-being.

And as I recall, the croquet wickets were left set up out in the big side yard, for the children to play with. Mr. Deacon's indoor hot water tub got finished, and took some getting used to, at least for me. I suppose prior to that I figured that the big back porch was somehow mine, reserved for my duties, to be suddenly cut down near in half. And of course when the tub was occupied by Mr. Deacon, at least two times a week, I couldn't go near the porch, and felt peculiar even being in the kitchen, a shy wall away.

Yes, things were dream-like, like I was moving through my own time while watching it from another, near helpless, excepting to eventually come to my terms with Mr. Finley. Things good and bad merged and mixed, as I myself couldn't rise to take a side. Stacy Kremer wrote to me, too, you see, and I couldn't even stir into a panic, not from his letter, which Elizabeth delivered to me, nor for his brief words, which told me of his intentions to speak to me in civilness, intending to visit the Deacon home once more.

Well, he arrived that very early afternoon, alone and on foot, and for the reasons I mentioned, without any great alarm on my part. Elizabeth saw different, though, for no men were about, save Little George. She quickly had Sarah and Emma summon him in from the stables, or tack shop, prior to allowing Mr. Kremer into the house.

Stacy Kremer, quietly and most patiently, obliged Mrs. Deacon, entering the stillness of the big house with his hat in his hand only after Little George was already seated in the parlor. Both men looked fearful, Little George of the duty assigned to him, and Stacy Kremer of something ghost-like that ate at him.

"Ladies," he began, and then fixed it, darting a sad look to Little George. "Ladies and sir, I come most gratefully, and sober as can be. I'm a frightened man, and ashamed to say so," he said, spreading it out to the three of us.

"Your business, sir?" Elizabeth asked softly.

"I've tried to lead a good farmer's life," he answered as soft, "but none is perfect."

And he went on some, of friends good and bad, of wise choices and poor ones, but mostly, and oddly, it was his dress for that visiting that I recall, all proper in checkered trousers and a matching vest and ascot tie. I of course was dressed as I did daily, but felt nothing of it for it was painfully clear that he had come begging for something none of us could give him.

Little George eased up in his silence as Elizabeth softened further, especially when Mr. Kremer's tears came silently to his eyes as he rambled on, ". . . two men dead and one dying, and the law at a loss," as he rubbed at his wool trousers.

I thought how I didn't even know this man before us, with his thinning hair all slicked so proper, and, by then, with his cheeks wet with his own despair, this man who more than once asked me for my hand. But I felt for him for a first, and I didn't rightly know why, but I felt my Christianity when he looked straight to me, and pleaded, as though no others were in the room, "Miss Waltz," he wept out, "Clara, will I be spared?"

And his shoulders shook and his chest heaved, and he put his own face to his hands, talking through them, "Oh, I'm burdened, Clara. I'm burdened with just sorrows and regrets, and with rightful fears."

"And so am I, Mr. Kremer, so am I," I answered him. "I'm sorry, but I don't have the answers for your questions, but I wish that I did," as my hatred for him melted away, for it was then that I first saw it, about the bones of his weeping eyes. Oh save me, how I did see Emma's own eyes, so clearly, in Stacy Kremer's. And I'd never tell her, not for years and years, not until after she was married off herself, and then only because she asked me.

Then he was gone, off on foot, as he had come. I last looked and saw his lone figure far up the farm road, heading toward town, or the Catawissa, I figured. But those dream-like days of that May must have been so only for myself, for Elizabeth, only days later, brought up to me her plans for a grand to-do, an anniversary party for she and Mr. Deacon in June. She was earnest and hushed, and for no reason, for no others were about.

"I don't want to wait for our twentieth, Clara," she told me as I tended to mending in the parlor, as she thumbed through one of her catalogs. "It'll be our fifteenth this June, and that's good enough for me."

"You must be very proud, Mrs. Deacon," I replied.

She never looked up. "Oh, we are, with the kids and the farm and all. It's all been so wonderful, and gone by so quick too. And having you and Emma come to us has been a blessing, too, for these past, oh my," she paused, "ten years now, is it?" she asked, looking up from her catalog.

"Almost ten, and thank you, Elizabeth. Thank you so much. I do need to hear such kindness for Emma and myself these days."

"Oh, you dear thing. The both of you, and especially you. It's been such a difficult spring."

"Worse than difficult, Elizabeth. Most dreadful."

"Let's talk of nicer things, Clara," her voice chippered. "You know, I may be out of line, and I may be very wrong, but," she dared a smile, "do I perceive a friendship between you and that nice Mr. Finley?"

That caught me off my guard as I darned at a pair of Joshua's stockings.

"Oh, Elizabeth, we're acquaintances to be sure," I told her, and I may have blushed, "but a couple in the coming? Oh no. He's just an awfully kind man. And some twenty years my senior as well."

She smiled. "My Henry, too, figures he might be seeing something, Clara."

I must have shied up further, for she finished the subject with, "I don't know, Clara, but a nice big party might be just the medicine for a budding romance."

And we talked on, with me changing the talk, and with Mrs. Deacon allowing it, but I did wonder over how it could have shown. And then I wondered more that evening, over that Mr. Mark Twain, or Samuel Clemons fellow, and if he ever thought of his perhaps imprisoning a person into folk-talk, turning him into a Johnny Appleseed who never wished to be. Then later that night, much later, I thought so silly of myself for even considering Mr. Finley for being that boy, all grown up. I thought how men such as Mr. Deacon were more right than myself about near everything, and it was a large land we lived in, with so many people, and what were the odds that HE'D ever show up about these parts, much less than ever take an interest in someone such as myself. Oh, I felt most foolish, I did.

So I consoled myself to my Scriptures that night, reading from several. I wound up, though, staying with Timothy. In Paul to Timothy I found sorrow with 5:4, "But if any widow has children or grandchildren, that these learn first to practice Godly devotion in their own households and to keep paying a due compensation to their parents and grandparents, for this is acceptable in God's sight." You see, the Deacons weren't truly family to me, and I lost my own mother to illness as I lost my father to my crime.

And my reading then went to widows left destitute, and about their placing their hopes with God. I pondered, in Timothy, those men, my attackers, where it mentioned men who wouldn't provide for those who are their own, and of their being worse than those without faith at all. Then I read more of widows, as I had the month before, of how they can become unoccupied, and meddlesome in the affairs of others, which returned me to myself, and my own thoughts of late. But I took pity on myself too, and righteous it was, for I only wanted something good to become of my Emma and me. And it was in Timothy 5:14 that this truth came to me, for it read: "Therefore, I desire the younger widows to marry, to bear children, to manage a household . . ."

* * *

Some time had passed, perhaps a week or so for it was still mid-May, and word had it that Joe Logan was still surviving. The stories varied, of course, but he was alive in all of them. And things lifted for me about the farm as well, for along came this one day to become such a nice one for this remembrance of that time.

My chores were light about the big house, and it was a fine and sunny day outside, and quiet too, for Elizabeth and the baby, were out and about somewhere. Mr. Deacon was up in the city and things were slow about the farm. Only several of the hands were about their work, and that was far from the big house. Mr. Finley himself was off fishing with Little George, Emma and Joshua. They took to the river before dawn, and as I cleaned and polished that morning I thought of them down there, beyond the Watsons' and that other large farm, both of which sprawled out over the land between the Catawissa Line and the river. I wondered what Hank Finley could have been thinking down amongst those same trees where he did what he did only five months before.

In time, the four of them came back just after the noon, with a heavy line of bullheads and two fine pike. And after the mid-day meal, Hank Finley most took me aback, asking of me, with a great deal of modesty, "Would you consider a leisurely walk with me, Miss Clara, if you could tolerate my company?"

He then pawed at loose dirt beneath him. I smiled to that.

"I'm agreeable, Mr. Finley," I told him, thinking of Mrs. Deacon's words, and wishing to not make a spectacle of ourselves. "A stroll would be nice."

* * *

So about midday off we wandered, with him leading the way, down along the one fencerow that led to the fields about Mill Creek.

After asking if I held any preference, to which I had none, we made our way upstream, quite shy of one another for it was different that time, for his asking, naturally. And he carried that old hat in his hand too, and his long hair I took notice was combed nice and slicked back. But I should talk, for my own hair, I saw to it, was brushed out and clipped back, and I put on a colorful apron that I favored back then.

Shortly, we come upon the beaver dam, and a nice slapping sounded out to our arrival. It was their tails you see, warning one another of visitors. And we stayed there a bit and pondered their work amidst all the chewed off stumps.

"Did you know, Clara, that they also scurry off and hide to the commotion of their own falling trees?"

"I didn't know that. It must be a funny sight," I answered him. "Why do they run off so?"

His nice old eyes surveyed the beavers' work. "That friend of mine, that I told you of before, he told me most probably due to the attention they fear they're drawing, and as I said before, he was a pretty learned feller."

"He the same man who fooled you regarding the true nature of rainbows?" I dared teasing him.

"The very same." Mr. Finley smiled broad. "The very same, Miss Clara." Then he looked to me and folded his bony hands before himself. "Mr. G. Witte was his name, out there in the middlewest. And a right curious feller he was."

Then we strolled on, farther up the Mill Stream, in the lower fields behind Sarah and Emma's schoolhouse and the paper mill beyond. And we talked of stories again and traded two new ones. His was of this man known as "The Woman-Hater of Blue Hill."

"His name was John something or another, and he lived thirty or forty years ago," he told me as I took note that we kept nearly in stride with one another as we walked. "And he built this little stone tower," he went on, "which leaned too, atop this Blue Hill summit, overlooking Sunbury, downriver on the Susquehanna."

"And he hated women?" I cut in.

"Even the sight of 'em," Mr. Finley nearly laughed, "and he kept loads of books and was right never seen without an umbrella. And folks claimed he could ice skate from Sunbury to Harrisburg in half a day, and did too, just for sport whenever the ice would bear 'im."

Then he paused, so I did too, where the creek turned. Then he said, "They say he died on a farm somewhere near the city. Williamsport, that is. And that he was buried, then dug up and reburied atop his Blue Hill the following winter. Strange feller on any account, wouldn't you say?"

"Yes, I would," I agreed. "It doesn't sound natural."

"Not natural a'tall, Miss Clara."

Then I wondered just then if the time was ripe to ask him for the story of himself, for who he was, that is, and from where he had come from, not for what I saw him do. But wishing more to preserve our time together, I asked instead, "You ever hear of the legend of Conrad's broom?"

"No, Miss Clara, I never have. Would you favor me with it?" He offered me his elbow at a slippery patch that I could have crossed alone.

I took his arm anyway, and it felt nice to do so. Then I did slip a bit, and I grasped tighter, feeling of his upper arm, strong for an older man, then I thought of that winter dawning, then I flustered, and looked about, so as not to be seen, of course. Then past that slippery patch I kept to his arm, for as I said, it felt nice, and no others were around, and then I told him young Conrad's tale.

"Was supposed to have happened, I believe, some hundred years ago, somewhere near McElhattan, south or west of Jersey Shore."

"I believe I've heard of the place," he said as he helped me. "Through a pass in the mountains."

"Well, a man named William Crispin died," I began, "leaving his widow, a woman from Selinsgrove, with their brood of youngsters. Conrad was their oldest, and he done well assuming what he could of his father's responsibilities. But by the time he was not but sixteen or so, he took a shining to the lone daughter of a queer German couple, the St. Galmeirs, and she was said to be beautiful, truly so, considering her odd parents."

"What was her name?" Mr. Finley cut in.

"Elizabeth, and she was said to be spooky too, but she hooked young Conrad in spite of it, and Conrad's mother was most suspicious of her strangeness, so she had Conrad invite her to their cabin for a big supper, figuring to hide a broom beneath her front steps, hearing that evil ones, or spirits or such, couldn't step over a broom."

He smiled to that, and I was pleased, so I went on. "Well, this young thing, she sensed the broom right off and demanded to have it removed, so young Conrad was quick about it for his affection for her, and he was also most angry with his mother. Anyway, they all ate and visited, behaving as though nothing had happened and in due time Conrad saw the young girl home, through the forest, but on their way she, well, she tempted him, I suppose." I shied up. "And they became intimate in the woods between, Conrad later shared. But the next morning was the story."

"Don't stop there, Clara." Mr. Finley smiled again, looking on ahead, while patting my hand that held to his elbow.

"Well, early the next morning," I added, "her queer old man of a father, the old man, St. Galmeir, showed up at the Crispins' home, all in a frenzy, claiming his Elizabeth was deathly ill. Conrad, of course, went to her immediately, and to his own horror he claimed that her face had changed and gone most ugly just over the night. She couldn't speak, but she did look to him, and just all full of sorrows, Conrad claimed."

Then I looked to Mr. Finley, and he looked to me, so I went on.

"Well, spirits or fever or whatever took her life by midday and neighbors were called over and all, for things was different then, Mr. Finley."

"Please, call me Hank," he asked me quietly as we strolled. Then he tried it out himself, looking kindly to me, "All right, Clara?"

"I'll try," I replied, before going on, nice and easy with, "Anyways, she was dressed and straightened and all, to all's fear over her new appearance, but it did no good, for she disappeared that very night."

"Her body, you mean?" Hank asked me.

"Yes, never to be seen again."

"What become of her folks?" he asked as a breeze stirred up around us.

"I guess they just lived on, all alone and just as spooky and queer, or more so, to those who lived around them back then."

"How 'bouts the boy, Conrad?"

The boy, I thought to myself. Didn't that just fit his curiosity? "Don't know. I suppose he just grew up. What do you think, Hank?" And it felt good using it too.

He laughed lightly to that as he stopped us. "Yes, Clara, boys just grow up, they do."

"We should turn now, don't you think?" I asked him.

And so we did, and we did so for a fine walk back. I recall that breeze too, for it stayed up, out of the west that clear blue afternoon. I also let go of his arm for I didn't wish us to be too familiar. "You don't mind, do you?" I asked him. "I'd be shy to be seen holding on to you."

"But not ashamed I hope?" he returned, most thoughtfully.

"No, Mr. Finley. Not at all."

And then we talked on as we strolled along that path, and I thought of his clothes, unbeknownst to him, for I knew them all by then, and of course I thought of the ones he picked for our walk, and of how they looked recently washed. I also wondered if he thought of mine, or knew of them the way I knew of his, and if he had favorites or anything.

By the time we got to the beaver dam, which was quiet, our talk lessened, but in a nice way as we traded shy glances and smiles to one another, like we had a secret between us. And I suppose we sort of did, for we laughed easily and all about us seemed friendly, if one can say such things of the weeds and the trees and the flowers and the birds.

Then our talk turned to affection, for maybe we both wished to know what the other knew about such business. And strolling along the lower field fencerow, leading into the bottoms, we talked of pain, of its nature and reason.

"Something I think we both know of, Miss Clara," was how he softened it for us.

Then affection came back, strengthening into love. "I never had one, Mr. Finley," I confessed, "Leastways never one that was returned to me," as I kept my gaze ahead of us.

"Well, I had a first, and an only one, Clara. But long gone now, and long ago," he claimed, and I believed him. Then he went on with, "A right lonesome walk, Clara, through the gateway of bein' grown up, I reckon."

I supposed a broken heart was surely a faster way of getting there, so I said so.

Then he stopped us by stopping himself along the edge of that lower field, and he took his hat off again, for he had put it back on as we turned to come back. He tried to slick back his hair again too, but it wouldn't go as nice, but of course I never said so. And it was then that he first asked me of anything of myself.

"Miss Clara, could I call on you? You know, all fitting and proper?"

"Oh me," was all I could say.

"Court ya, ma'am, like a gentleman, if you'd have it."

"Oh, Mr. Finley, I just don't know."

"I'm sorry. I truly am if I'm embarrassing you. If ya wish, Clara, we can say no more and none will ever know that I asked—"

"First, how about that story of yourself, Mr. Hank Finley?" I come out with, surprising even myself.

"Perhaps some day, Clara, and I truly mean that, I truly do."

"Well then, I'll think on the other, Mr. Finley, and I truly mean that too. I truly do," I answered him.

And then the wind must have died down, or maybe it picked up, for I recall being able to smell of him just then, faint in the afternoon, that nice smell of his that I felt sometime before, upon a wagon ride.

And then we walked on back, saying little to one another, but feeling nice about it all.

CHAPTER 11

And then I thought of myself as silly and foolish for all my adventurous ponderings over who he really might be, and especially so after his wanting to call on me and all. In those same days another of my turns came around for caring for Mrs. Snyder, and it proved to be both harder and easier, for I fancied I had, like a proper girl, a courting man, to fetch me home when I was to be relieved. I also figured that some of his prior escorting me to and from Mrs. Snyder's had been a courting of sorts already anyway, and that too made me feel as nice as I could, considering, of course, what I also knew of him.

But as it turned out, I had to see myself to the city, but it was no matter, for Mr. Finley was to come for me in three days, on Deacon business of course. And it was again Rebecca who I relieved, and true to her busyness she had much to say, and she began it with the state of Joe Logan's health.

"My James got it firsthand," she claimed, "from close friends of a Williamsport constable. Poor Joe's awake at last," she stated as if she knew him. "And he's even gotten steadier with his stretches of wakefulness and sleep. Almost near regular."

And she went on too, as I settled in for my stay. She talked of the Williamsport constables being disappointed of Joe's not being able to recall any of his beating, nor nothing of his attacker.

"Simply nothing." Rebecca was urgent. "Like those hours were to him what Mrs. Snyder's life is to her."

I thought different, of course, to that comparison, but said nothing. Then she went on about the Deacon anniversary party, then much in planning. "How wonderful and beautiful and joyous it'll all be. Don't you think so, Clara?" she asked, before sighing, "Oh course I'll be just weeks off from birthing, myself. What a sight I'll be!"

"Well, they're wonderful people, and they deserve such an event," I agreed, and meant it. But I also had my own thoughts on it, thoughts more toward Elizabeth's own speculation of an event such as that being something of a nice time for the likes of Mr. Finley and myself as well. Of course we'd have to work in anything of that sort, about our own duties and responsibilities for that evening.

Then James showed up to retrieve his swollen wife, and to a touch of my sadness he would show up again, two days later, informing me that I'd have to show myself home the following day, for Mr. Finley had Deacon business to attend to. I caught myself being silently angry over it, and even a touch sore at Henry Deacon too. Oh me oh my, was I getting soft for him, I was.

Then only a day after my return to the farm things got shook up a touch once more. And, to boot, I had only seen Mr. Finley but once since my return, and that was from across a distance.

This next event took place at a family dinner, all regular, save the attendance of Reverend Ashhurst. And I recall the one topic of their conversation being the proposed notion of a borough water system.

"No, no, Elizabeth," Mr. Deacon corrected his curious wife, "for up in the main part of town."

As for myself, from what I took in, I imagined it as wonderful. No hand pumping, just the turning of a lever and you have it. Water, like magic. Yes, that Constable Keeler was right, modern times was upon us.

Another of their topics was the history of Muncy, downriver, and Mr. Deacon was quite eager to relate some of which he had recently become fascinated with. As for myself, I'd been there only a handful of times, and knew little of the town. It only brought frightened Stacy Kremer to my mind, for his farm, I understood, laid west across the river from that town.

"Originally, it was Fort Muncy, Reverend, and one of the farthest outposts into the wilderness up the Susquehanna River," Henry Deacon spoke as he ate.

"Wasn't it destroyed once, though?" asked the reverend.

"Yes, and then ordered rebuilt and fortified in the months that followed the slaughter at Wyoming," Mr. Deacon said as he broke off some bread. "A man named Colonel Hartley received that new command, and he didn't care for it much, preferring to fight the more orderly British over the savages roaming the dense forests. The Revolution was well into its second year by then."

"How did he fare, dear?" Elizabeth knew to ask.

"He rebuilt the fort," Henry Deacon swelled, happy to go on. "He ordered her restocked, then took men, I don't recall how many, and headed up through our own parts here, then struck north, up Lycoming Creek, crossing the northern mountains. I imagine he then found the Tioga, because he and his men then routed several savage villages along the Chemong River before heading east to destroy several more out toward Wyoming. They're after coal out there these days."

"A perilous journey," the good reverend observed as the talk of ". . . up Lycoming Creek . . ." my own home, was still with me when we heard horses trotting up the farmhouse road.

Our meal was wrapped up quick to the courteous arrival of big Amos Reese, accompanied by that Constable Keeler and his quiet constable companion.

I saw to their arrival, of course, and Amos was quite friendly upon the veranda, which calmed all, especially myself. Then Little George and Hank Finley were summoned up from the bottoms, or from wherever they were at the time. That alarmed me, the Hank Finley part.

But all stayed most cordial inside for the wait. Then with the arrival of first, Little George, then Hank Finley, Amos asked Mr. Deacon and all else, save the children, "Could I have everyone in the parlor, please? For just a brief exchange of any knowledge anyone may have regarding two visitations here at your home, Mr. Deacon?"

So we all filed in and seated ourselves. Then Amos began it, and kindly so, looking to me longest, and most sincerely, as he informed all in the parlor, "This is just a general fact finding thing—nothing to be nervous over, my friends." Then he breathed deep. "It's been now near half a year since the first killing took place down along the river, and the law's still searching, but that's no secret. To that end," then he paused and readjusted his great

size, "we're here this evening to inquire of what exactly tran-
spired with two separate visitations that occurred here within
your home, Henry," as he ended it, looking of course to Mr.
Deacon, who was smoking, occupying his own chair.

Then the constables, that Mr. Keeler, and then Harold Reese
himself, each took their turns in asking us all sorts of questions
over the visiting of Joseph Logan and Stacy Kremer that time
back when they had been drinking, and then more over the second, lone visiting of Stacy Kremer, when he was so fearful and
forlorn and all.

The quiet deputy hardly said a word, save answering Elizabeth Deacon's sole concern of, "How is Mr. Logan faring, if we
may?" she asked at one point.

"He ain't outta' the woods, ma'am," was all his stillness said.
Outside of that he only tossed a certain look here or there.

And to my relief that Mr. Keeler didn't pay me much mind at
all, as all three stayed mainly interested in every little thing said
and done, or even hinted at across both of those visits. Things
wouldn't get rocky until Constable Keeler pressed Little George
on some point that I can't recall anymore. Little George feared
up quick, and unexpectedly, taking all in the parlor quite by surprise, save for that Constable Keeler himself.

"I think you know more than that, George," the Williamsport
constable pressed him. "Don't you now?"

"Why you only on me, sir?" Little George sang out fast and
scared. "What's any of this gots to do with me?"

"It's my seasoned feeling is all, George. Put into a question
for you."

"It's her you're after!" Little George cried out, pointing to
me, taking all in the parlor aback. "She's the one for your questions, sir! I tell ya, you all had your dogs up the right tree months
before, ya did. But ya gived up on her too soon!"

"Lordy be, Little George," cut in Mr. Finley. "What are you
up in a fever over?" Then he grinned wide. "Why, everyone figures the killer to have been a big man. A big, strong man, George.
Probably right clever too, bein' that he's still out of the law's

good reaching. Them things ain't you, George. Not by a mile, they ain't."

Then all smiled and laughed most lightly, save Little George, who stayed fast to his seat, huffing and puffing. Even that Mr. Keeler's mouth broke into a smiling appreciation for George's fear. And before the hour was up all three men were gone, and soon things about the Deacon house returned to normal, with me at my cleaning up dinner, and the others to their pleasures. And as I worked, with Emma at my side, I silently thanked Hank Finley in my heart for cutting off Little George as he had. But still it worried me, it did, with Little George thinking what he was thinking.

And as I worked that night, and then later, as I took to our bed to sleep, I thought more about it and I knew I was going to try to get Mr. Finley to tell me more, but I never thought, save me, I never thought that I'd do it so soon. Nor did I think that night that I would get all of him the very next day.

* * *

That next day began sunny, but a fast rain came through late in the morning. It stayed near an hour, and hard too, but near as quick, the sun came back and shined bright and sparkly upon all the wetness that still laid all over.

Well, I ran into Hank Finley just after the noon meal, and we agreed to have ourselves a walk, mid-afternoon, and I did so look forward to it, for my worry over the constables visiting the night before and all. So I busied up my duties, and then I tidied myself and brushed out my hair, then I tied it back, for I wasn't happy with any of my bonnets while trying to make myself most presentable. Then Mr. Finley and I met up out in the big side yard, caring some not to be seen, but not hiding either.

Mr. Finley must have thought to tidy himself as well, for he looked most handsome in a white shirt beneath a vest I had seen little of, and he was carrying his hat so as one could see his greased back hair. And he was freshly shaved too, for spots of drying blood marked the one side of his neck.

Well, we made our way together walking near the same walk we shared before, down through the bottoms and out toward the Mill Stream, to follow it out past the beaver dams. I didn't take his arm and he didn't offer it, but I didn't need it either, for it was so nice and sunny out, and the air was fresh and clean and most nice to breathe from after that morning's fast rain. Even the birds did seem to liven to the day, and I commented on them and their pretty songs.

Mr. Finley kept his smile closed-mouth, as I had taken notice of lately, back then. I learned later that he had become shy over several missing teeth. It made no sense for I'd noticed them long before, but he did it nonetheless.

"Cause they're singin' don't mean they're getting' along, Clara. They're fitful, they are," he said as he looked up to them, as we walked side by side.

"How so, Mr. Finley?"

"Hank, please. You can call me Hank. They're warnin' each other, about us and about themselves. Constantly taking claims, to trees, to branches, fence posts and on and on, wherever they're at. Wanting each other to stay away from each other."

"Your friend again, Hank?" I asked, and I felt good about it.

"Well, yes, probably so," he answered me, as his smile finally broke. Then he changed our talk, and his smile too. To something softer, asking me, "Miss Clara, have ya thought much about our last talk?"

"I have. I have, indeed, Hank," I said, as I looked straight ahead as we strolled, as a cloud passed overhead.

Then we came upon the Mill Stream, and it was running high and cold looking, and I mentioned that.

"This morning's rain, Miss Clara. The Loyalsock'll pick up her load this evening."

Then he paused, and he didn't smile. "Would ya consider company such as mine?" he asked, turning and looking straight to me.

"Yes. Yes, I would," I answered him, "for I've come to be fond of our times together, Mr. Finley." Then I braved up with, "But I do need that story of yourself first off. Please don't ask me why, for I can't give it to you. I surely can't, Mr. Finley."

"Oh, Clara, I'd promise it to ya, but you'd—"

"I'm going to tell you something, Mr. Finley," I cut in as we strolled again, "and it's something that I've never told a soul, and I never will." My voice then shook. "And there's much to say over that too, Mr. Finley, Hank, for all I've been through this past spring."

"Go on, then. Please do, Clara."

"I think you may be someone other than who you say you are," my voice quivered. "And I care for you, I do, and I fear I care for you in a womanly way, and I also know something that has continued to frighten me, all my very life these past five months."

"Go on with it, Clara," he said, his kindness returned to me.

And we stopped then, both of us. It was sunny again, and the air was cool and moving as I went on, "Horace Wills, Mr. Finley. It's Horace Wills." And I started to cry. "The morning he died he was searching for a woman amongst those riverbank trees. Only three people know that—me, an ignorant man-child, and the one who," I cried harder, "oh, Hank, the one who ended his days amongst us."

And then I near lost myself as I clutched hard at his nice vest. "The woman he sought, Mr. Finley, was me! Oh Hank, it was me he was chasing through those trees that early morning. All over again I feared, and I hid from him, inside a big old dead tree that had fallen. Oh, Mr. Finley, I saw his killer, I did, and I do so care for him, I do."

Then he grabbed me back.

"Clara," he said hard to my face. "Clara!"

But at long last it was out of me, and oh my, it felt so good. "I'll never tell, Hank. Not ever. I'll never tell a—"

"Clara, let me talk," he said to me, pulling me closer.

Then we both calmed some, but not much, in each other's shaking grips.

And then I was out with the other.

"You're him, aren't you? You're the grown-up man of Huckleberry Finn! Aren't you, Hank?" I cried to him in that breeze.

Then softly, he told me, "Let me give you that story, Clara Waltz, that story of myself. It ain't long. No, it ain't too long."

And then he told me that tale of himself. And I cried more too, but I loved him for it, from that afternoon on, for the rest of his life.

* * *

"Miss Clara," his old voice came out with, "I was born two years beyond fifty years ago, out in Missouri. My given name at my birth was Henry Jacob Finn."

Then he looked about sadly, and then straight to me with his kind face, with them flecks of his dried blood still on his clean shaved neck. Then he asked me, "Are your Huck Finn suspicions shared by any others about?"

"No, Mr. Finley. I'm quite alone with the notion, as I am with near everything else, and ashamed of it all as well."

Then his kind face smiled to me as he wiped at my tears with his handkerchief. "You're not the first to figure such a thing, but you are, Clara Waltz, most certainly the kindest, and the most gentlest of 'em."

I still held to him as he tucked away his handkerchief, and lightly took hold of my back. "I had a light-hearted father, Clara," he began that story. "Yes, my pap was. Never took to workin' either, my pap, not for wages leastways. But he was light-hearted, he was, and anyways, by my second anniversary, I was told, by both he and my mother . . ." I felt his grip then tighten on me.

"Go on, Hank. My Mr. Finley." I smiled; I'm sure my face all wet. "Go on."

"Well, Clara, sometime, when I was still little, he took to calling me, Huckleberry. Huckleberry, as a baby. And then, Huckleberry, as a little boy and beyond."

CHAPTER 12

And we stood there, we did, holding onto one another amongst the new spring weeds along the Mill Stream.

And his big Adam's apple worked so then, with the both of us breathing so hard. I reached up and flecked the dried blood spots from his neck for some reason.

"You've got to believe me, Clara," he said first. "You've got to in order for you to understand just why I drowned that Horace Wills feller."

I nodded. It was all I could do. Then I told him softly, "Tell me why. And tell me all about yourself too."

So he gently worked us apart and placed my hand in his arm as we began that most memorable stroll of ours, up along that thick and rippling Mill Stream, that wet and sunny spring afternoon.

* * *

"Clara Waltz, not a thread of what all I'm about to tell you will be an untruth," he began his tale of himself. "Not a single thread of it. First off, Clara, I lived out there, along that river, and I was that boy."

Then he breathed deep. "That Mr. Mark Twain feller, he fiddled with the times some, I do believe," Hank told me, patting my hand, which clung to his arm. "Learned people puts it, I've heard, cause I've taken to listening in, Clara, whenever I come upon talk of the tale, that it was supposed to have taken place in the forties, such as that book writer's own childhood. But it weren't so, Clara. At leastways not mine and Jim's big float."

Then he straightened his tattered hat as we walked, and I whispered, "Go on, Hank. I've waited so long."

"We did ours, which'n the tale is told after, in the fifties. Summer of fifty-four. But that storybook, Clara, is all right by me, for it's mostly a tale, as I said already. Just with me and Jim and Tommy Sawyer in it and all."

"Did you ever read it, Hank?"

"No, ma'am," he said as he smiled. "But I can read, I can. I did start to one time, but it seemed most silly to me. And it made me sad and angry too, not long into it, for how he had me talkin' of my pap early on in the book."

"How so?" I asked, looking to him.

"My pap was taken by liquor, Clara, and hard and heavy, but he was all right for awhile. And of course, he was my pap, and no one else's."

I tugged at that colorful apron I wore for him, to tidy myself. "I never read the book either," I told him, "but meant to with my suspicions and all."

He was silent, so I went on, "One needn't read the story anyway, for it's most popular and most folks have the general idea anyway."

But he stayed quiet, so I asked him, "Tell me of your pap. We can start there."

"Miss Clara," he answered me as we strolled slow. "He was a light-hearted man, as I said. Too much so I've come to reckon, bein' an old feller myself and all."

Then I squeezed his arm and he brightened, "You see, I was eleven or twelve years by then, when all that happened, with my runnin' off with the Watson slave and all. And my pap was a drunkard too. But he weren't always so, but that Mr. Twain didn't concern himself over that, or any more about my family. And again, and truly so, that's all right by me. It truly is. I've got no quarrel with any of it. But to the truth of it, we was poor people who lived in one cabin or another along the Mississippi. Not many minded our squatting, if anyone even owned the land that we hunted and fished upon to begin with."

We came upon the beaver dam about then, and we paused to admire it amongst the higher water, with me still holding to him. Then he went on.

"And as I said, my pap never took to regular workin' for wages and all." And here he looked so kindly to me. "And I guess my mother was of the same stock, for my memory of her is a kind one, her as happy and loving, for I was already of eight or nine years of age when she passed. She died birthing, Clara. Alone with my pap, in the middle of an awful starry night, for I went out into it as a boy, fearful of her cries, and of my pap's desperation which I was old enough to see in him."

Then he made like he was surveying that woody length of the beavers' toil before he went on. "It was a girl. She birthed herself a baby girl. Stillborn, I reckon, or dead shortly thereafter. My mother died not long after, about sunup as I recall. It was about them times, Clara, that my pap took to drinkin' so, in his sorrows, and I stayed with him for I was just a child myself. But time did us both in, for his drinkin' ways stayed with him, and truthfully, Clara, he weren't ever any good any more after that."

"I'm sorry for you, Hank. I truly am," I told him as we both looked out across the beaver lodges, I do believe they call them.

"Oh, don't be, Miss Clara. It was all so long ago. He did die, though, my pap. He drowned, not murdered as told in the storybook, I heard tell, while Jim and I were out on the river them months. I also heard that men," he quickened, "learned men, who ponder such things, were disappointed with how that Mr. Mark Twain ended his book."

"I haven't heard that, Hank. But I'm only around learned folks about the Deacons' table, and that subject hasn't come up."

"Well, it might be as fitting as most any other part from what I've come to gather. It happened to us. Probably not as colorful and adventurous as writ, but Tommy Sawyer did show up, and we did lose and then find Jim again, and of course the river itself did have to end," he said as he smiled, which made me smile too. "It's right simple enough for me," he went on. "I reckon Mr. Mark Twain wrote that storybook just to spin a right good yarn, and of course to get himself good and rich over it," he said with a pleasant laugh, which comforted me further.

Then he fixed his hat and patted my hand. "You look most pretty today, Clara."

I shied up. "Oh my. Thank you. You look very nice yourself, Mr. Finley. Shall we walk on?" I asked him.

"Yes, we should."

And we did, side-by-side, and somber once more as he began his other tale, one of fifteen years—of why he killed Horace Wills' horse, and then Horace Wills himself.

* * *

We made our way slowly along the fencerows above the beaver dams, to where the Mill Creek turned northward, at the base of that wooded hill that rose up behind the farmlands that sprawled out behind our small town. Amongst that growth, Hank got to that woman he lived with, the one he mentioned before, who wouldn't be his wife through her own wishing. All said up to that point was of the remainder of his lonesome boyhood, lonesome as I saw it leastways, with my arm laced through his as we strode slow, through and about the creek-side weeds and thicket.

"She was regular odd, Miss Clara. Different, Annie was, as I might of told you before, I believe."

"What was her family name?" I asked him as we neared the open wooden bridge, the one for the road north, the road Loyalsock Avenue turned into back at the edge of town.

"Payne. Annie Payne was her whole name. And I took on livin' with her and her little boy, Robbie, in my twenty-eighth year or so, back in '70 or '71," he recalled thoughtfully.

"So he'd be in his twenties now," I offered. "Her boy, that is."

"No. He's gone too, Clara. But he was such a good boy, Robbie was, such a good little boy. And as I stated before, he weren't mine, because I came along after, and Annie never did tell me who his father might'a been. She knew, though, she did. But it was painful to her, and I never cared enough about it to pester her for it."

I watched the road before us, wondering at first, then knowing quite sure that I'd keep my arm through his if someone came along. But no one was in sight, save a carriage far off, heading away from us, up the Loyalsock way. I noticed that birds were about too, in great numbers around the base of that wooded hill as I told him, "Go on with it. I'm listening."

"Well, I was with her for several years, about six miles or so upriver from Cincinnati. We lived off the north bank of the Ohio River. Her, good ole Annie," he smiled off, "her boy, Robbie, and me. And we got used to each other pretty quick, tending to our own needs."

"She never bore you a child?" my curiosity prodded.

"No, ma'am, and to be right truthful, we weren't that way with one another for the longest while, Miss Clara. But we did work out to become so, in time. And I was happy for it because I was fond of her. You would have liked her. Her, and the way she spoke and thought over things and all. She was tall too, a gangling thing, but I told you that before, didn't I?"

"Yes. Yes, you did. And I listened too, Hank Finley."

By then we emerged upon the open dirt road north, so we walked to the bridge that crossed the Mill Stream and stood upon its planks to decide which way to walk to from there. It was a nice break for Mr. Finley to fuss over his hair as I straightened my dress and favorite apron. Then both of us looked down through the open planks of the bridge at the water that tumbled beneath us, before deciding to keep to the road, to head back into town from there. We had nothing to be shy about, we also decided, and then laughed over it quietly.

Returning to his tale, Hank told me, "Well, we were something of a little family and all, and had been for a few years by 1875. I was thirty-three or so. Annie, late twenties somewheres. I worked for wages, but only when we needed the money for cabin supplies, and that was but three or four times per year, 'specially prior to the winters. You would'a liked her, though, Clara."

"I believe I would have, if you did," I told him, thinking too on how I was keeping to his arm as we left the little bridge behind us.

And of course he went on, and it was a most terrible tale, indeed.

"Well, Robbie and me, we was off huntin' early one morning, and got back just about the noon of the day. Little Robbie, that nice boy, with his big bucked teeth and all. Well, he was somewhere behind me, toting rabbits and a duck as I entered our cabin alone. And well, Miss Clara Waltz," he said as he stopped us upon that dirt road, looking through a streak of sorrow that come up from somewhere within him. "There was men there, inside our cabin. Five of them. And they was doing to Annie what those men had done to you. And I swear to you, Clara, I swear to you that one of 'em for sure, you and poor Annie had most sadly shared."

He took a good hold of me then, and I didn't mind it either.

"Clara, listen to me now," he nearly whispered.

"I am, Hank. I am."

"I tried to stop them, and I tried to hurt them, but all happened too quick and too wild. I was beaten, and badly. Annie, she was beaten worse, added with their other crimes, which left her as half naked as they had her when I walked in on 'em. Oh, and she was wild and bloodied in the ruckus which followed—a ruckus she and I was losing at, and one which ceased with the entry of little Robbie, just a little boy, standin' there in the doorway, strainin', holdin' up my rifle."

"Go on, please, Hank."

"Clara, one man went for 'im, and halfway got 'im, just as the rifle went off."

Then he paused, for the words were hard ones.

"Well, poor little Robbie, in trying to save us, he blowed half his own head off."

I shuddered and Hank took another firm hold of me, reminding me, "Fifteen years has passed since then, Clara." Then he went on.

"The men, they scrambled of course. And Annie, oh, that dear woman, she went for her Robbie, and he of course was dead in moments more. Well, it was a terrible time to live through, and

Annie, poor Annie was broken forevermore. She didn't wish to, or couldn't part with little Robbie's remains. It took a whole day for me just to get her dressed again. Her torn clothes and her half nakedness just didn't seem to occur to her. Her speech too somehow left her, and Clara, I never, not ever heard her say another sensible word, 'cepting for her crying out at nights, in the dark, from dreams I reckoned, ones she could never share with another soul."

"Didn't you seek help?" I asked him. "There had to be others about."

"Oh, yes. I got help from folks along the river, folks such as ourselves," he told me as I took notice of a lone rider approaching in the distance. Mr. Finley must have seen him too, for he loosened his arm for my sake, but I kept his escort, I did, content with it all.

"Our help, Clara," he continued, "saw to my getting little Robbie buried all proper, and seeing to it that the law was after what had happened to us in that cabin. Oh, they were sad awful days. I still think of 'em sometimes, Clara. Especially, this one slow moving picture of poor Annie sobbing, her long arms and hands bloodied, rocking little Robbie, clutching to him so, tryin' every once in a while to fit that bloody piece of hair clinging to his skull back onto the one side of his dear little head."

I shuddered again. Then I noticed the rider who was nearly upon us. I knew him, but not his name. He used to sell dry goods up in town, but I didn't know what he did anymore. He tipped his hat and looked us over, for my being who I was, I was sure. You see, my name got around a good deal earlier that winter. I cared none though, keeping to Mr. Finley's arm in his nice loose shirt.

"Go on, Hank," I asked him.

"Well, I stayed on with Annie, in our cabin, and I cared for her for over half the new year, but she never changed, Miss Clara. Never and not a bit. She never ate a thing, less'in I fed her like a baby. And she never cleaned herself or dressed herself or anything, just stared off all day, day in and day out, only to cry out in her fitful sleep most nights, week after week, and on and on." Then he paused, looking out toward the bluish rise of that last mountain of our Bald Eagle Ridge that rose up in the distance before us.

"If it's too difficult, Hank, I'll understand," I told him.

"It's all right," he answered me. "Dead by now. Long since dead by now. She has to be. They took her away, these people of hers, once they got the news, and the last I heard she was put in the asylum for the insane, just built back then, downriver in Cincinnati. But she's sure to be dead by now. Gravely ill, Miss Clara. She was most gravely ill."

"I'm sorry for you, Hank. I truly am," I offered. "Is there more?"

"Yes, there is. I stayed on, Clara, because it was my home too by then, and behold a single year later this storybook comes out, in '76 or so, called *The Adventures of Tom Sawyer*. And, well, we riverbank folk, 'specially us that stayed put for considerable stretches, we did get to know one another, and of course most knew me to have come from them parts on the Mississippi. And it was a mighty coincidence to all of 'em along the Ohio back then that there was a Huck Finn boy in that storybook."

Then his mood differed, not as somber.

"I did claim to be that boy, or the notion of that boy that the book writer, Mr. Twain, had used, after hearing about the tale, and seeing it as a string of events very common to some that I had gone through with a small tribe of other boys, and most particularly, a boy by the name of Tom Sawyer. I figure my claim got around some, and for the worse of some people, and especially with this one feller, 'cause it grew with this notion that perhaps I kilt Annie's boy, and made all else up. No one ever saw those pillaging men, these people argued. And it was said to be broad daylight, said so by me. And this talk grew, Clara, and people with a mob sort of mind begun to come about, nosing around over it, so I packed light one night, and just wandered away."

In my listening, I recalled those boys and that dog on the road to Muncy. Men, like boys, and in a small mob, and especially so after he reminded me that Miss Payne was there long before he was and was known to those folks.

And then he went on with his life after that as mostly peaceful as we strolled closer to the edge of town. He told me how his life changed mainly twice, due mostly to that story, of men claiming he was a liar, and of others wanting to fight him, just to say they did it. And the story of the dead boy, too, haunted him as it spread in its own ways of how people talk. Then he told me of how that other story came out in 1885, the Huckleberry Finn one, just five years before that stroll of ours, and of how it drove him from the South as a fabled nigger lover. "So I wandered north, calling myself Hank Finley, and it's fooled all thus far, Miss Waltz, 'cepting you," he said as he patted my hand on his arm.

And of course I'll never forget his words as we both heard the bleating of Earl Marshall's sheep, just up Loyalsock Avenue ahead of us.

"And then I couldn't believe it was happening, Clara," he tightened, "that icy cold morning, to come upon that stranger amongst those bare trees, with him askin' me of his lost kid sister that he sought along that riverbank. Him with his red hair and his harelipped mouth, not knowing that I remembered him to be the same man who had halfway gotten to poor little Robbie in that doorway a spread of years before."

* * *

Hank Finley didn't kill Charlie Logan, nor did he beat Charlie's younger brother, Joseph, into the simpleness that his injuries made of him, nor did he have any idea of who might have done those two deeds. He told me so as we walked, and I believed him as the bleating of Earl Marshall's sheep faded off behind us that spring day.

And those days of that late May warmed for me, they did, for Hank's truth over who he really was, and for how he did indeed hold affection for me. At long last, perhaps I too could become something to someone.

And so of course I was agreeable to courting, but I was also shy about it, I was, wishing to be prudent and modest over it. Hank felt likewise, so we learned about smiles across distances, nice looks across the big lawn, or the holding pens, or up the house road. We learned of how nice those affectionate looks could be, and oh me oh my, of how much a soul could say with them.

Those days were kind ones to me, regardless of the events around the farm or beyond. There was planning to be done and arrangements to be made, for the big party in some four weeks to come. Elizabeth was most thoughtful over it, not nervous or worried or anything, such as she could get over other dinner parties. She seemed warmer with those preparations, satisfied somehow, as though the reason for the big get together was reason enough not to fret. And even news, which should have been worrisome, didn't trouble me as it would have before.

You see, word came, from Rebecca, or from her husband, that Joseph Logan fell ill with the lockjaw, on top of his other sufferings. As for me, I truly felt that it just wasn't any of my concern anymore. I prayed over it I did, but I couldn't suffer for it. And I prayed more when word came proper, from big Amos' handsome son-in-law, that it was indeed true. And sad too, as young John Thomas told Mr. Deacon of it, for Joe could have fought the lockjaw, you see, if he was healthy, and with fitting medicines, and if it was known soon enough. But "healthy" was the word he stressed, for as it come to be, Joseph was left simple, as I told before, save he grew worse off in time. John Thomas also reported that the doctors said they couldn't be certain that his beating even gave him the illness to begin with. They said sometimes a man can get it and not know from where or how, for even the tiniest of cuts can be enough. But near all agreed it had to be his beating, and I figured the same, for it was said that although beaten mostly about his head, he was still opened up quite a bit. And as I wrote before, I did pray for him, I did, for it was most proper to do.

And it rained more too, but the sun was never far off, for Mr. Finley and I began a daily walk, early in the evenings, as a way of our early courting. And I supposed it was noticed too, but none said a word, not farmhands, nor neighbors, not even my Emma, leastways not to me. And from those rains the river and the creeks rose, and the logs were cast off for harvest in the big booms, which had most talking, for lack of other subjects, as I myself, reflected upon my own hollow log, my sudden shelter down there amongst those riverbank trees, that were by then surely greening over. And I wondered, I did, of how it'd feel to go back down there, knowing what I knew and all.

Over tending a nice supper, I then learned that James Snyder's new tannery was doing well, and that he was most hard at it trying to make it a success. Then all of us learned that Stacy Kremer was questioned again, at his own farm it was reckoned, down between Muncy and Montgomery. But none knew if the questioning was of the light kind, or of the hard and enduring sort. I, of course, said nothing, but not out of fear anymore. I was simply drained of it, and I also felt a growing distance between myself and the thoughts of the others over all of it.

Yes, they were nice kind days for a change. While upon one of our evening walks, I asked Mr. Finley what he figured of his boyhood friend turning out to become a United States congressman and all. And, oh my, what pleasant thoughts he had. They were brief, but like most of his ponderings, they reached good and far.

"Oh, Miss Clara," he answered me, "he was a talker as a boy, boastful and fun at the same time. A popular boy too, with young and old alike," as he kicked a small rock off the road, smiling softly. "Yes, I reckon him to be a windy one as a grown man as well. So," he paused, then continued, "I suppose the House of our Congress to be a right comfortable home for him. Carpetbaggers, one in all, those fellers."

"Do you suppose he ever wonders of you, and what may have become of you?" I asked him as we strolled.

"Oh, I've heard things, I have, as you have, and all else too, but a body never knows for sure. Seen some in print, so I reckon he has wondered of me, whenever asked about us as youngsters, or as grown-ups, which occurs, I understand, from time to time."

* * *

Yes, those were nice days, those last weeks of that May.

Over another nice supper, with Reverend Ashhurst in attendance, I recall happy and easy talk of the big anniversary party to come. The good reverend quoted Scripture.

"From Hebrews, my friends," he announced thoughtfully, " 'Let marriage be honorable among all,' and none have exemplified that sentiment more righteously than you two," he toasted Mr. and Mrs. Deacon, who lightly kissed at one another, then humbly smiled for all about.

It was all done so warm and kind that I looked up the passage myself, much later, in my bed with Emma. And there was more, there was, and not fitting for the table. Then I thought of, Mr. Finley before I slept, then I dreamed of him too, sometime that night.

* * *

And on our walks those spring days, Hank Finley and I also talked, most quietly, of that other business, the killings, for we weren't without our concerns.

I figured both groups of those men to be circus people, but Hank couldn't recall if a big show was about back then in Ohio, when his friend was attacked so, and when her little boy lost his life. And I secretly showed him Charlie's photograph, which I clipped from the *Gazette* months back. Charlie could have been amongst them, but Hank wasn't certain as he claimed he'd rather be. Of course, Joseph, ailing into dying at the time, couldn't have been. At Hank's and Miss Payne's sad time, he was still up Lycoming Creek, and the apple of my girlhood thoughts, with me carving out soap bars and such for his attention. But I did hang on to the notion of circus men, for all of mine were, save for Stacy Kremer. But Mr. Finley didn't care to ponder it as much as I had, so I left him alone over it, but it troubled me to do so.

It troubled me for I needed to talk to anyone about what happened to me, and then at long last I found someone, in Mr. Finley, who knew of such a horrible thing as what had befallen myself. I needed him, or anyone, to share with me the aching truth of what I felt for so long, and about how none of it was truly worse than any of the other, the hitting, the shouting, the laughter, and of course, that repeating pain. None, you see, seemed to me to be the worst, only that it all happened to me, as a single evil doing. And of course I needed to talk of how I then carried two babies, one a sorrow, the other a blessing. I desired back then that Mr. Finley could hear me over it, but perhaps he wasn't ready, nor ever would be, or could be.

And Mr. Finley and I continued our daily walks, amongst more preparations for the Deacon anniversary party, toward May's end. And once or twice, we even rode the new safety bicycles as well. On one walk too, we strolled up into town, before the buggy and sleigh builder's shop. I listened as Hank told me, "I'd like to learn a craftsmanship such as that one day, Clara. A man such as he leaves something behind, something useful, and to his credit."

"You wish to make a mark, do you, Mr. Finley?" I answered him.

"Yes, I would, Clara." He smiled. "Do you think I've got the time to do so, at my age and all?"

"Yes, I do. You've got plenty of time." I smiled back. "Which brings me to your thoughts for the reverend's words. I speak of the blessing he gave, Mr. Finley. From Hebrews, he prayed for us, 13:4, which read: 'Let marriage be honorable among all, and the marriage bed be without defilement, for God will judge fornicators and adulterers.' "

Perhaps he figured I was measuring him. Fine by me, for I surely was. His answer, though, was slow, but thoughtful, like most else.

"Good words, Miss Clara. Fine words. Words which, if taken to heart, and to livin', would go a right long way toward not complicating a body's long days, I'd say," he said with that nice smile, right to my eyes.

I looked to him too, and I didn't look away. So he added, "A whole big book full of good notions, Miss Clara, that Bible of yours is."

And he looked thoughtful to me too. And I thought we might even kiss right then, but we didn't.

* * *

Then two pieces of news came at May's end, one a single day after the other. The first came from John Thomas, Amos' handsome part-time deputy constable, and full-time laborer and son-in-law. I learned from Mrs. Deacon that he told Mr. Deacon of Stacy Kremer's leaving his own farm, of which he took such pride, and the Susquehanna Valley as well. John Thomas' talk had it that Stacy Kremer left his farm to neighbors, and to his aged father to tend to, as he himself headed south, for the Gettysburg area. Others claimed beyond, to distant family in Maryland.

Then the other news came, from Amos' other part-time deputy constable, the thin nervous one, Harold Elmer. Then it came again, the very next day, printed in the *Gazette*, and all read of it. The lockjaw had gotten Joseph Logan, for he had passed away during a fitful deep sleep.

Most all talked of it, talk and whisperings of convulsions and spasms of the body whilst one's starving to death. Convulsions and fever tripped off to the voices of beloved family about, and worse ones to the sight of sunlight mistakenly allowed into his darkened room. Thoughts which moved me to pray over him, one more time.

CHAPTER 13

The *Gazette* ran its story of Joseph's dying in the first week of that June. It was a big front-page story. "Late Night Attack Becomes Fourth Killing!" their headline hailed. Titled beneath, in smaller print, was: "Stalker Still Among Us—Valley Remains in the Grips of Fear."

I read those stories, along with a couple of others, about one killing or another, each supposing who the killer might be and all. I also read them when alone, for I remained shy over all of it, even amongst the Deacons.

That same week school let out for the summer as well, and I looked forward to having the youngsters about the big house and yard over those early summer days. Then another turn of mine came up to care for Mrs. Snyder, which I didn't mind, for it got me away from the farm and our town, when near all were making a new fuss over the fourth murdering. And I also looked forward to the big anniversary party preparations, which would occupy myself upon my return.

But my safe haven up there in Mrs. Snyder's silent home wouldn't last. Two days into my care I was summoned back, to endure another questioning. A friend of Rebecca's, who I didn't know, showed up quite alone, carrying a small bag, to relieve me, looking at me as though I was scary. And it wasn't Mr. Finley who was sent to retrieve me either, which scared me worse. It was Little George, all in a fluster, telling me right there in Mrs. Snyder's own parlor, "Mr. Deacon wants you home, Clara! At the request of Amos Reese, and them Williamsport constables."

"What for, George?" I asked as I stole a look to Rebecca's friend, whose name I'd learn on my way home was Miss Wallace, once a grammar school teacher, but no more.

"For interrogatin', Miss Clara, and believe me, ma'am, that it ain't on no account of myself. I ain't said a word no more to no one. Not to a soul, Miss Clara," he huffed and puffed, not caring if that Miss Wallace was listening in or not.

I cared, though, for the way she watched at the both of us, but I'd care no more once on the Deacon carriage, heading home, through the Market Square to be exact, when Little George told me that they were questioning Hank Finley himself. "And hard at it, Miss Clara, mighty hard at it," he added.

I feared for why they chose him, and for how he'd stand up. The first had to be for our being seen together as of late back then, in ways other than Deacon family duties. And as I said, I feared for how he'd stand up, especially if they were being as cruel to him as they were toward me. After all, he was guilty of the first one, and I didn't know if he could cling to a lie. He was a man to his own purposeful loneliness to be sure, with his hidden real self and all, but that wasn't exactly a bold-face lie told directly to hard questioning men such as those constables, and especially that Constable Keeler and how he could be.

Well, to my further fear, Little George took me directly to Amos' office, without time for stopping at the farm, for my room, for tidying up, as were his instructions Little George told me. At Amos's office there was also no sign of Mr. Finley about, nor any of his having been there, save for an empty chair against the very wall that those men once had me to. I also didn't know what to look for anyway, but still I looked, even searching the faces of Amos Reese, that Constable Keeler and his silent partner. Only in the face of Amos' handsome son-in-law, John Thomas Moon, did I detect something other than hardness. He looked shaky, and I never learned why.

As it turned out they went quite light on me, keeping me to that chair for three quarters of the hour. Constable Keeler and big Amos alike questioned me mostly over my friendship with Mr. Finley. They were mostly interested in how long I had known him, and since when had we been keeping company with one another. Then they grew keenly inquisitive over just how much Mr. Finley knew of my own past, after I let it out my own self, commenting on our both being lonely souls. Then abruptly I was dismissed to Little George, who I found waiting nervously outside.

I wouldn't see Hank Finley for another day, for he was off on some duty Henry Deacon had assigned to him. That alone frightened me, for I worried over what they might have gotten out of him, until kind Elizabeth, the next morning, shooed the youngsters away from the big house kitchen as I was whipping up griddle cakes. She wished to share what she learned from Mr. Deacon the night before. And oh me oh my, they must have been hard on him.

"For upwards of three hours they kept him to that chair," Elizabeth told me.

I shuddered, and stilled, from my whisking.

"Do you need to sit, Clara?" Elizabeth asked me.

"No. Please go on."

"Well, Henry himself," she whispered for no good reason, "couldn't stand being in the same room, for his fondness for Hank, but had to be for some official reason or another.

"That Mr. Keeler," she went on, "he screamed and hollered and swore blue streaks about the room, and up in Hank's own face as well. And do you know what, Clara?" she asked, then told me, "Your friend, that Hank Finley, he never so much as shook a quiver, Henry told me."

I relaxed to that, working at my batter.

"Henry told me that Mr. Finley just sat there in that chair and answered their questions as though they were concerned over a feeding, or a turning of one of the fields, bless his soul."

Then she went on, leaning forward with a smile, "And he even owned up to his affections for you too, staring so calmly right back at that mean constable, right to his eyes, Henry told me, telling them of his offer to court you, and how he'd be a right lucky man if you allowed it."

I must have shied up, for Elizabeth commented, "You're blushing, Clara. Mr. Finley's a kind man, and your friendship's honorable and fitting."

"I do need to hear that, Mrs. Deacon," I told her, although I did feel shameful for her having to be fooled, along with all else, with the part of that business that happened down there amongst those riverbank trees.

Then she went on with it, putting together all the pieces she could. At one point Constable Keeler lit into Hank about Williamsport's being the lumbering capital of the entire nation, not some dusty, two-jackass collection of cabins somewhere out west or down south, or wherever it was that Hank said he was from. The constable went on to say that even Montoursville now had two sawmills, a paper mill, and a chair and table factory, along with a brand spanking new school building.

Hank reminded him, at that point, and to Mr. Keeler's displeasure, that our town's hook and ladder company disbanded back in '87, due to a lack of activity, and that neither Montoursville nor Williamsport was a Baltimore or a Philadelphia by a long shot.

"Was he angry, Elizabeth?" I interrupted her.

"I don't think so. He just told them that they could cut down all the trees in all the world and sell them for all the money in the world, and that that wouldn't make either himself nor you, Clara, a killer, nor friends of such people. One had nothing to do with the other to his calm reckoning," Elizabeth told me as I stoked the fire for my batter.

Then she asked me for more tea, and I poured us both another cup as she again shooed away Sarah and Joshua.

"They're just hungry, Elizabeth," I told her.

"They can wait another minute. Neither are starving," she quickened. "Anyway, Mr. Keeler then screamed and cussed some more," she earnestly hushed. "And to Henry's shock at the constable's deportment, that Mr. Keeler then claimed he could stand no more of Mr. Finley's presence, and ordered all from the office, excepting Amos and my own Henry, who were both ordered to '. . . take no statement from the man!' "

Of course, I myself could readily see that scene in my own head.

"Well, Amos and my Henry remained, and stayed both silent and motionless as instructed, Henry told me. Hank Finley did the same," Elizabeth nearly whispered. "And then, after near half an hour had passed, a lone little mouse scampered out onto the floor, picking at the men's crumbs as it paddled itself to and fro, nearing Hank Finley's own crossed feet.

"Then Hank Finley spoke, 'We're in here with you, little critter,' he said, breaking that long silence."

Facing the warmth of the stove, I believe I smiled, for I could see that as well.

"Then that mouse jumped a foot," Elizabeth continued, "taking flight to a corner it must have been used to, for it was gone in a moment.

" 'Near blind they are,' Hank said to neither of the men in particular. 'A man I once knew, a right curious man, told me they'll climb right up your own trouser leg if a body sits and stays dead calm about it.'

"Then, neither my Henry nor Amos said a word, but Hank Finley did. 'Brings Miss Clara to mind, don't it,' he said again to neither of them. 'Near blind as a child she must a been. A blind young sheep of a young girl, leading her own self to wolves. Now here we are, some dozen years after, and wolves are upon her again. Righteous ones this time around.' "

"He shouldn't have," I said still facing my batter.

"Well, the other men returned shortly after that," Elizabeth continued. "And your Mr. Finley was dismissed."

"I like the 'your'," I spoke soft, then turned to her.

Elizabeth smiled to that, perhaps proud of herself, then went on, "Well the men talked some, once alone," as she sipped at her hot tea, "I suppose while waiting for yourself being brought to them by Little George. Henry said that the silent Williamsport constable figured Hank might just be their man, for he didn't so much as quiver throughout all. 'He's brave enough, and patient enough,' the silent one figured. But that Keeler thought otherwise. 'The codger's smitten with the Waltz girl for sure, but it's not him,' he told the men, 'lessen he runs on us shortly,' he added, looking to my Henry."

Of course, the whole thing welled up in me as I told Elizabeth the griddle was ready. And it scared me some too, for if he could lie as he had to them, then what about to me?

Then Mrs. Deacon quickly changed her posture, both inside and out, as she could so lightly do. She rose, and called in the children, then turned to me and smiled sharp, as she said, "You won't see *your* Mr. Finley most of today, Clara. He asked Henry for the afternoon off. Some business he has in the city." She smiled again. "Little George told me," she leaned toward me, "that he's getting himself cleaned of the tapeworm with some strong medicines from this doctor in Williamsport that Doc Raymonds doesn't have. He's preening for you, woman," Elizabeth whispered, then winked.

* * *

As for the days that followed, I can't recall much of the suspicion business, but I do remember a good deal of our preparations for the big anniversary party, for it was just around the corner on the calendar. And it was on all's mind about the Deacon big house and farm. I recall the weather was most fine too, for Elizabeth fretted over it, and for good reason. She and Mr. Deacon were expecting upwards of one hundred guests.

Of course I was to work it, as were the other hands. In fact, Elizabeth hired on another four more for the day of the festivities, as well as a small musical troupe for the big dinner and the dancing to follow.

For my own evening apparel, oh how I wished so to pretty myself up, doing the best I could with what I had. I had a nice dress, but nothing at the height of the fashion of the day. My formal bodice was of that "V" design with short sleeves and a swag of lace wrapping around my bosom and shoulders. I had no train with my overskirt of faille, which was split in front and pulled toward the back with swags and poufs ending at the hem. My bustle was what gave me trouble, though, for I used my best, which was quite out of date. The bustles at the time were of that sort which appeared near separate from the body, as though on wheels behind those most fashionable ladies. Mine, you see, was of the older style, which rode higher on the back, beginning above the waist a good deal. Well, I tried to reform my nice older one, and I thought at the time that I did a proper working of it. To top my appearance off, I bought long gloves up in town, and borrowed, from Elizabeth, tiny earrings and a bracelet, which she insisted upon, wanting me to present myself just right. And of course I was to work as well, and that favorite colorful apron of mine wouldn't do, so I also purchased a pretty tea apron while I got my gloves. It had a gathered drawstring neck, which tied in the back. It was made of sheer lace with embroidery and pastel satin ribbons for the trimming.

And oh me oh my, how I looked forward to seeing how Mr. Finley would present his kind old self that early afternoon for the party's beginning. And he did himself well, too, for who he was and all. I was spreading the last of the tablecloths when I first saw him, and he looked right fine, as though a gentleman himself. His trousers and vest were of dark gray plaid wool. He also wore that billowy white shirt for the second time that I saw up to then, and he wore it with an ascot tie.

When I complimented him over his appearance he told me, "I've got a regular Mackintosh straight coat, but no proper cape as the other men'll be wearing after the evening grows cool."

"Where's that tattered hat of yours?" I teased him.

He smiled then, and nice too. "I'm savin' it, Miss Clara, for a more proper occasion." Then he reached for my hand, as though to shake it like a man's. But instead he held it between both of his, and he told me, "Lovely, Miss Clara. You're the loveliest one here now, and I'll bet for across the evenin' to come."

"Oh, please," I replied, for I didn't know what to say. Then I put my free hand atop our hands. "Thank you, Hank. Thank you very much." Then I added, "You could use a nifty derby or a bowler hat, Mr. Finley," I chided, happy with myself, "but then I couldn't see that nicely slicked-back hair of yours."

Then the first of the guests began arriving, and we were ready for them with most of our labors over, across the past days. I myself cooked next to nothing, as two of the hired-on help saw to that large task.

Croquet started the afternoon off, and oh what joyous sporting contests unfolded across that sunny day. Phonograph listening, too, kept many upon the Deacons' front verandah. As for myself, and my Emma, we happily served the guests, enjoying such an occasion for all the splendor it brought out in the guests.

Of course not all played the games, or rode the bicycles. In fact, near half simply shared fellowship in conversation with friends, both old and new. I recall one elder man's stories of times long past, and of how they were a changing so. "Used to be, back when I was a boy," he went on, "that it took near a whole week to get to Pittsburgh or to Philadelphia. Why today it'd take you, what, fifteen hours or so on the busier rails? And to even cross the Atlantic nowadays, they can steam her in less than ten days."

Another older man heartily agreed. "Telegraph poles and lines, they're all over nowadays, like the canals and the railroads, hardly anywhere, leastways in the east, where they don't reach."

At another circling of men, it was the Grange they wrangled over. "Used to be over eight hundred thousand strong, not but fifteen years ago. Near a political party itself, I tell you." But I caught little of it, for I was watching my Emma, dressed as finely as myself, then my kind Mr. Finley, looking so genteel, carrying a silver tray about, with drinks and handkerchiefs for the guests.

Others talked of the celebrating hosts, my employers themselves. I overheard of their wedded life, the sharing of one another's sorrows as well as joys. ". . . blessed with sturdy children . . ." and ". . . so faithfully observing their sacred vows . . ." then "finest of people, those Deacons . . ." In the parlor, where I caught up with my listening-in Emma, the elder ladies, from both Montoursville and the city, bantered happily over "Tea Town," Montoursville's old nickname.

"It came from the woman folk sending their men off to the city for tea and coffee by the half pound, I tell you, Mary Ellen. And I should know best. I was already this old when you were still cackling nonsense, girl," one of them said to the rise of gay laughter.

The other, this Mary Ellen, huffed back, feigning great displeasure, "I'll agree with your age, old woman, but it was men on the road between Muncy and the city who stopped here for rest when this town was nothing fit for decent folks." All laughed again, as I myself, though, I thought of that dog and those boys on that very road. That was my pain, you see. It was never far away. Then I noticed Emma looking at me, maybe wondering where my own smile went.

But all in all, it was a grand time before the great feast to come, with folks young and old listening to one another with great interest over merry incidents, past and present. It gave one the kindliest of feelings, it did.

Then the Reverend Ashhurst quickly announced, "Ladies and gentlemen! Refreshments, one and all! In the form of a most bounteous spread of food! Please, let us be seated, one and all!"

And so it was that near one hundred of us did sit together that afternoon before great roasts of beef and venison, and oh me oh my, so much more, all prepared by the skillful hands of those hired-on women before Reverend Ashhurst rose again, bringing all to order and silence for a most fervent blessing out there in that warm June sun.

And what a thoughtful prayer he offered, after shaking hands long with Mr. and Mrs. Deacon. His affections for the both of them came through strong from his solemn words. He began with how he wasn't present when their nuptials were performed, and he continued with words over what a privilege it was for he, and for all of us to be in attendance upon the anniversary of the marriage of two such fine Christians. His earnest thoughts from his bowed head touched upon the parents of both Henry and Elizabeth, both couples from farms upriver, in Piatt Township, where Henry and Elizabeth first met as mere children, along the banks of Pine Run. ". . . a beautiful little rivulet that meandered through the fields of both families' farms . . ." Then his prayer hardened, following their voyage through life, ". . . a loving providence, earned bounties from past labors, and the dreams of those yet to come . . ." He hailed their reputations as industrious, honest and temperate. Then his thoughts quieted, going back to parents, Mr. Deacon's own, ". . . deceased, amongst other beloved friends and neighbors who've been called to eternity." And I strayed off then, and shouldn't have, but I did, thinking of my own mother, and both folks of Mr. Hank Finley, all gone for the pastures of Heaven.

And then I raised my head and opened my eyes to look for him. And I saw him, opposite from me, across the crowded tables upon the lawn, and he looked so handsome to me, strong for his age and thinness, even a might dangerous, and that was evil of me, it was.

The reverend's words were just a blur to me, I suppose, as Mr. Finley then looked to me too, and smiled to me across all the bowed heads and bonnets, before bowing his own head in a nodding way, his own way of reminding me to do the same. So I did, but not for listening to the reverend's righteous words. I bowed my head and thought warmly of that special friend of mine on that so special day.

Then the reverend was done and our town doctor, Dr. Paul Raymonds, beckoned all's attention for a poem he wished to recite. I liked that Doc Raymonds. He was a kindly soul, quiet, and the only one I knew back then who didn't mention Williamsport as "the city." I think he knew well of much larger ones, and perhaps even quietly wished to live off in one of them but for some reason couldn't. And his poem was pretty, of love and of children and of the purest of pleasures, and of life's too few treasures. And then the big meal began, and what a feast fit for the occasion it was.

I enjoyed serving the victuals to my appointed tables, as did Emma, I learned later. Most all were more than kind to me as I worked, considering that I didn't know half of them, and considering that most of them had all at least heard of me. And I listened in to table conversations as well. One happy couple was that spring breaking a large lot for themselves somewhere up the Loyalsock Creek. Another man held Reverend Ashhurst's table spellbound with his earnest discussion of religion about the world.

"Only a century ago," the man went strong, "the Papal power was so proud and defiant. Now our Protestant influence is gaining on her even in Europe," he assured all who listened. But my recollections fade here, they do. They fade off for the sundown and the evening which followed. The games, that gay musical troupe, all the strung-up kerosene lanterns that so beautifully lit the big Deacon lawn for the fine dancing, and the antics of the children about.

Yes, it was that evening that I'll never forget. As for we help, our responsibilities lightened so we could socialize too, which we did. I even felt as though I was one of the ladies, in my gown of sorts, and with my hair all done up and all. At least I felt so for a while, and it was a nice while too, amongst the Deacons' proper friends.

Best though was when Mr. Finley took me aback, asking me to accompany him upon the lawn for a dance of our own. Well, I didn't know what to do, so I let him take my tray, then lead me out there amongst the others. And when the music began, we tried our best we did, and it was wonderful. I'm sure we looked to be a sight to the others, but none said anything then, leastways not to us and not for a while.

Well, we danced several more times, amongst our duties, and each was better than the one before. I'm sure I didn't look anything like the ladies about us who swept so beautifully about the dark lawn, in the arms of their men in that soft light of the lanterns. But we did dance, and he did hold me, and I did so feel for him. Mostly to me now, though, it was our faces being so close and for so long to the nice music. That closeup staring that dancing allows. I suppose the first times are the best in their way, due to permission's sake and all.

The only sad point to the entire evening, and it wouldn't spoil a single thing for me, was when I was in the pantry, to my duties again, midway into the evening. I forget now what I was fetching, but I had trouble finding it, which kept me in there. Well, I then heard my name said, by a woman in this group of them just outside the door. And it was said in a nasty way too, so

I stayed in there, quiet and still, hoping not to be discovered, and hoping they'd go away. Then my name was said again, and to another round of their gaiety. And it was Rebecca Snyder's voice, which hurt just a bit. She had them reflecting upon my dress, you see, and then more over my bustle, which as I said, wasn't fit for the fashion of the time.

I felt bad, I did, but mostly for Hank Finley, should he hear anything of my being unfit for the occasion.

Then more was said, by another in their group who I knew from church. Her name was Kathleen, but most called her Kitty. She was answered in turn by the voice of that last girl to relieve me of my duties at Mrs. Snyder's, that Miss Wallace, who seemed to be afraid of me then. Her talk was over how we, Mr. Finley and myself, had dared to go out and dance amongst the others. "How forward and assuming of them," she hissed and then laughed, as did the others.

In a short time, I suppose, they were gone, for I recall being out of the pantry and shortly amongst the others. I said nothing of it to Mr. Finley, of course, for he did say earlier that I looked so nice, and I did wish him to think it so.

Well, about ten o'clock or so the presents were brought out, and they were most elegant and costly-looking to me. By ten-thirty, or thereabout, the doxology was sung, followed by another thoughtful prayer, a benediction by Reverend Ashhurst, and then there was good-natured handshaking and warm farewells all around.

Some left promptly, for a special hired-out coach on the Catawissa Line, bound for Williamsport. Others, though, lingered about, for it truly was too delightful an evening to take leave from. As for myself and Mr. Hank Finley, and only after permission from Elizabeth Deacon, we took ourselves another walk into that wonderful night. And as with the dancing, I'll never forget it. I'll forever hold that dark and starry stroll dear to me.

It's the business of none, other than Mr. Finley's and my own, that stroll was, but for this tale I do feel a need to relate bits of it.

We wound up down near the Mill Stream again, but not as far up as the beaver dams. And as I said, it was a dark and an awfully starry night, and I held to his arm too, at times with both my hands. And we talked of many things, we did, but what remains with me most was our talk of the crime that had happened to his friend Annie, and then years later to me. So much was similar, you see, save for her attackers were strangers. She had to fear for her life, you see, but not me. I knew my criminals, save for that one, who I'd later learn at least the name of. Unlike Miss Payne's, my death came to me as a ghostly, living thing, the death of my prospects back then, and of my very spirit for so long after.

Then Hank Finley and I quietly wound up near the laboring hands' cottages. Then we found ourselves amongst their outbuilding and tack shop. And in time, we turned ourselves from there, returning for the far off pretty lantern lights that still lit the Deacons' lawn, off across the near pastures.

We didn't mean to be so silent but we must have been, for we came upon two people, in a romancing position. They saw us too, but none said a word as Mr. Finley and I walked on. It was James Snyder, with that "Kitty" woman from church, the woman who laughed with her friends earlier that evening over my dressing and dancing. I thought of Rebecca, so large with James' child, and then I thought a mean thing, and felt most evil, for it wasn't Christian of me, but then again, neither was I that night as well.

But I prayed over it, I did, not asking forgiveness, just understanding, for Hank and I were both very shy and very simple over it, yet equally happy and quiet over it as well. Yes, I believed that then as I still do now, just as clear and pure as I can recall that nice smell of his, and the cool grass beneath us, with the stars so far above, as lovingly and warmly as I remember the knuckles of his bony hand that I kissed at when we stilled ourselves.

* * *

Well, in those weeks that followed the Deacon's big anniversary party, Mr. Finley and I did, indeed, begin keeping warm company. And it was very nice, and it was certain and quiet and understood.

It took most of two days to clean up and put away and to return the borrowed after that big night. I do recall that. And warm days they were, making for light times for Hank and I, with Emma included. I thought happier things, regardless of what others thought. Elizabeth Deacon also shared with me, from her staying glow from the party, how she found Mr. Finley's and my togetherness so nice and proper and springlike. She also told me, "My Henry feels likewise, but he's not the sort to comment about such nice things."

"He's not upset by us, is he, Elizabeth?" I asked her.

"Not at all. I think he even feels responsible for it, you know, by hiring Mr. Finley on and all. You know, Lord of the manor stuff and all that," she whispered, smiling wide.

One night in those same days, while reading from the Book Of Romans to Emma, I got to thinking of Mr. Finley's loneliness, and I felt needed for it, to smooth it away for him. The verse was 4:17, and it read: "None of us, in fact, lives with regard to himself only, and no one dies with regard to himself only . . ." It pained me to think of him as so all alone for so long, and not even able to be who he really was. At least I had the Deacons, you see, for Emma and myself. And, of course, I also had my Emma all the while, and my Scriptures as well, to console me.

Also, in those warm days, while about our duties and responsibilities, Mr. Finley's and my companionship had us riding the older high wheelers, pitching horseshoes and playing croquet, all left out from the party and for the summer. And we talked too, of things closer to us, things such as his childhood and mine, but more over his, and where all he'd been across the time since, and it did impress me, making me feel childlike in comparison.

"Don't feel that way, Clara," he told me, "a body can travel mighty far and never leave their farm or town. In fact, most rightwise people I've come across have deep roots, having never left their own valleys, farms and families. I've also come to learn that many of the wanderin' sorts can be fools."

I told him, amongst other things, "Well, I for one, secretly wish to travel way upriver, to Renova one day, to take my leisure like the fine folks do."

"You do?" he smiled. "Same moon, same stars, Clara. We share more than you think we do with them fine folks of yours."

* * *

Then late one night in that time, as we sat together upon the veranda swing, we talked of the spooky ring that circled the near full moon that night in the sky above us.

"I don't like it, not one bit," I told him.

"I don't know what it is, Clara. Seen it before, though."

"How about your curious friend?"

"Mr. Witte? Never heard him comment on it, of its making or meaning. I do find it pretty, though."

"Not me. To me it's a harbinger of things to come," I told him. "For I can take no more."

To that he smiled, and swallowed with that big Adam's apple of his. Then he snuggled my arm tighter into his. "We got to plan the things we can, Clara, and take the rest a day at a time."

And then one day, so suddenly in that early June, he was gone, said to have taken a leave of two days from his duties. But it turned out to be three, and that frightened me.

But I shouldn't have feared, not one bit. As it turned out, Hank had dressed himself up to travel by horse, a Deacon gelding, alone, up Lycoming Creek, to Cogan Station, to visit with my father, for I didn't know what. Oh me oh my, what a simple creature I was.

Upon his return he told me of two separate meetings with my father, and then another with Pastor English, which surprised me. We were sitting upon the veranda swing again.

"Your father and I," he went solemn, "we spoke of many things, of labor, and of men's duty to one's self and to all else."

I was quiet, but asked, "Did he speak of me?"

"Only when pressed, Clara. But he favored lumberin', and the nature of flood-stranded animals, ones ordinarily wild but near tame to the touch, as though partly dead with their fear."

"And of me?" I nearly whispered.

"He wouldn't, Clara, or couldn't. But I can. Do you remember our fishin' with the youngsters back in the early spring below the federal dam? That first nice talk of ours?"

"With us sitting on the rocks, as the youngsters downstream had a fire going?"

"Yes, that time."

"I remember it."

"Well, so do I, 'specially your asking me if I wished for the story of yourself. That pushed me, Clara, into knowing what I already knew."

Then he tugged at holding my hand.

"What did you already know, Hank?"

"How I felt for you, and how I wished for this togetherness, and how I'm such an older man with not as much to offer a younger woman."

Then he brought up a most terrible notion, cutting me off, but I didn't know what to say anyway, and he begged for my forgiveness for even pondering it, as he told me how he found my father to be such a fit and strong man for his years, which were well beyond Hank's own back then. And then he reminded me of my father's cruel disposition in regards to any talking of my circumstances, or myself.

"He seems to me," he near whispered on the swing, "to be a man, Clara, very able, and maybe of the heart, to do the harm what was done, is all I'm suggestin'."

"Oh no, Hank, he'd have to love me to do that," I came out with.

"It was only a thought, Miss Clara, only a thought. Nothin' more I can tell you," he kindly reminded me.

And he begged me to forget it, and I said that I would. But I couldn't, not easily, until, simple creature that I was, Hank Finley then added, "Your father, Clara, claims not to be the man to ask, in regard to having your hand in marriage."

I swallowed hard myself, taken aback. Two lone small clouds slid by that spooky moon.

"So I asked old man, Pastor English, and then the Reverend Ashhurst and then Mr. Deacon, and all three consented, with their best of wishes."

And then he asked me.

"Would you be an old man's wife, Clara? I love you like I've never loved anything before."

"Yes, I would, Hank," I told him. "I will marry you, but your wandering will cease, for I'll never let you go. Not ever."

He stayed silent, and swallowed hard again in that moonlight, but I knew what to do. I turned his face to mine, and I kissed him.

* * *

That very night in my excitement I allowed Emma to stay awake, as I searched for a consent of my own. And I found it in the first of Corinthians, from the eternal wisdom of Jesus himself. In verses 7:13-14, I read over and again: ". . . and a woman who has an unbelieving husband, and yet he is agreeable to dwelling with her, let her not leave her husband. For the unbelieving husband is sanctified in relation to his wife."

I found it at last. I could do something, you see. I could save him, as he was saving me.

"Emma, dear," I disturbed her, "put up your pictures of your elephants and lions. I have something for you to read."

And she read it and she said it was nice, but she said no more, save for, "You know the circus is coming, Mama, and soon, but I don't know when. We're going, aren't we?"

"Yes, of course, we'll go," I comforted her, not thinking of the big show, due in by rail, to Williamsport, in less than a fortnight.

CHAPTER 14

All smoothed gently for us in those first weeks of June. Only my Emma suffered any over that suspicion business, and that'd be up upon the grounds of that fine new school building that was just being built up in town, on Montour street.

They were naughty youngsters who teased her of her mother's being a suspect to the killings. I calmed her at home over it, reminding her of how some folks can be. Then I told her that I had news for her, and good news at that. "What is it?" she brightened, in our little room.

"Mr. Hank Finley asked me to marry him. What do you think of that?"

"What did you say to him?" Her smile tightened as her voice lowered.

"I told him yes, honey, for I'd like to marry him."

Then her smile vanished with a look of concern.

"We'll get a home of our own, Emma. We'll become a family of our own. Not right away, for we'll stay with the Deacons for a while, but after some planning we'll leave, and we'll need you, honey, to help us."

She smiled again, and then her concern returned. "Will he be my father, Mama? Will I have a father?"

"Yes, honey. And he so much wants to be your father. Will you let him?" I asked as I hugged at her, surprising myself.

Then she hugged me back, seeming unable to talk, which pleased me, it did.

* * *

And I also learned, from a letter sent to Reverend Ashhurst from my old pastor, Pastor English, that Pastor English and Hank Finley, at Hank's request, visited Ellie's grave. Pastor English wrote that Hank might be a righteous man after all, for he knelt softly in the high grass before her stone, and asked her, not praying, mind you, but not ashamed either, to come to me, her mother, maybe in my sleep to tell me that she was okay, and that he was too. His sort of faith I figured.

And I had another duty with old Mrs. Snyder in that piece of time, and it was a pleasant one too, for her frail old self did seem a little more alert. Perhaps her eyes were more clear than her usual eyes of fog, or maybe the warmer weather agreed with her circulation or something, but she did seem different, so I found myself talking to her more in that silence of her home. I even got silly and clever with it, telling her of my friend in waiting as I spooned her soup to her mouth, and cleaned at her face. Then I told her, "He goes by Mr. Hank Finley, Mrs. Snyder."

Then I whispered to her closely, "But he's really Huckleberry Finn. That boy, Mrs. Snyder, all grown up. And he chose me. Me, to be his bride."

And then I thought she smiled just a twitch, and that startled me. But it must have been my breath so close upon her face, for she locked away quick, back into her stillness.

Then I thought of her youngest son, James, and of that "Kitty" woman, and then of his unknowing wife, Rebecca, and I was thankful that her poor old self was safe from any knowledge of that sort.

Then it came time to be relieved of that duty after three days and two nights with her, and it was Mr. Hank Finley who came for me, and we didn't have to secretly manage it anymore, silently arranging that togetherness of escort. Our keeping company with one another had become common knowledge, and that felt most right.

So we rode home that day, eastbound through the city in the older open carriage, with Mr. Finley having no other responsibilities to attend to. And in the east end, still on Third Street, not quite to Faxon, we happened upon a house sale, and stopped and tied the gentler gelding to a post. It must have been a couple of houses, for there were tables of goods spread across two or three of those little front yards on that stretch of the road.

Well, we strolled amongst the goods, with my arm through his, and I recalled how I felt not but three months before, and of how it truly came to be for me and for us. Then at one table we separated, for his wishing to look over tools of some sort, so I browsed on, through used dresses, then silverware and dishes, before coming upon a table of children's toys and parlor knick-knacks, where I then near froze to the sight of them, off on a far corner of a little table.

All went quiet to me, the sounds of the women gabbing, the horse-drawn traffic behind me, even the play of the children and the birds about, for there they were, before my very eyes. Worn some, but there, the miracle of being there. Those soap-cake love-birds that I so lovingly carved out myself as the heart-struck child that I was way back then.

I looked across the tables to Hank. He was talking to this woman, I guessed over a price. Then I picked them up and carefully held my soap-cake lovebirds, my gift to Joseph Logan when just a boy himself, him then dead as I stood in that shaded little front yard. It was truly as though they had found their way home to me, it was.

Well, of course I bought them.

"Where did you get these?" I shyly asked the woman tending the table.

"Either my niece or my nephew. I'm not certain. It was years ago, though, ma'am, up in Newberry," she answered kindly. "We never bathed with 'em. They're too pretty," she added.

"Yes, they are," I answered her, thinking of Newberry, Joe's home, and Joe's end.

Once back in our carriage, and not until east of Faxon, while crossing the quiet farmlands west of the Sand Hill, I properly gave them to Hank Finley.

"These fit us, Mr. Finley," I told him, with my eyes straight ahead.

He held them, and turned them about, and momentarily I fretted. Then he answered me. "Why, thank you, Clara. Yes, they do. They fit us quite right. I'm a fortunate man, I am."

I also didn't tell him where they really came from. It wouldn't have been fair by him. But they made me wonder they did, about my long-gone baby Ellie, and of Mr. Finley's words of prayer to her. So I prayed back to her as our carriage worked across those farmlands, and I thanked her right.

* * *

I don't recall much else prior to our all loading up so excitedly, bound for the circus, once it rolled into the city late in June. Hardly any at all, save Mr. Finley's keeping company with myself, for our companionship became warm indeed, with his quiet smile, his soft gray hair, his kind words and of course his nice bony hands.

Then the circus rolled into the city by rail, and that was all the talk. And more bills sprung up, fresh ones, as far downriver as Muncy, and as far upriver as Jersey Shore. They showed up on trees, fences and on the sides of roadside barns and sheds. For three days the big show was to stay, with general entertainment by the afternoons, and with the big main events each evening, beneath their big top.

As all else were, we too about the Deacon home and farm were all in a lather over it, planning to attend the second evening's show, all of us together, up and back on the Catawissa.

And what a day and an evening it did start out to be. The kids were big-eyed and antsy across that day, in anticipation for the acts they longed to see. And with the baby in the care of Amos' wife, we boarded the train for Williamsport, arriving in due time to stroll amongst the sideshow acts and exhibits, prior to the main event. The only thing we missed was the opening day spectacle, the big parade about town on the day of the big show's arrival.

Once there we separated out, with Emma and little Joshua staying with Hank and I, as Sarah took off with Allison and Alexandra Rakestraw, while Mr. and Mrs. Deacon had the evening to themselves. Little Joshua preferred this, we learned. "Shall we be eating candy, Mr. Finley?" he asked.

"Sweets and treats, little boy. Sweets and treats," Hank said as he smiled, taking his little hand. Hank was about this circus business like a child himself, he was.

So we strolled amongst the animals in cages, and amongst those on tethers and heavier collars, the monkeys, Hank's camels and Emma's elephants. We saw the fire-eaters again, and I so hoped that we'd miss that tongueless woman, for she scared me. There were freak animals too, five-legged things, mainly dogs and cows. And there were clowns about, playing in their silent ways for the children. And then, as I had wandered over prior, we came upon them again, those men who claimed to be Huckleberry Finn and his colored man friend, Jim. They had an open half-tent of their own, between fat lady twins and something called the gator pit.

Well, a small crowd was assembled, and I coaxed Mr. Finley, "Come on, Hank, it'll be fun this time."

"It's those same fellers, huh?" He smiled, not like those months before. "Maybe it will, Miss Clara. Maybe so."

So I smiled back to him, and put my arm in his and held to him tight. "It will be, Hank," I whispered. "Just see." And I felt it so too, for I alone had the real one beside me, and he had asked me for my hand, and so we had each other.

And oh my, was I ever smart and sassy to that stomping-about circus actor. He was still barefoot and all, I suppose for the convincing. I felt though, this time around, for that tired looking old colored man posing himself as Jim, the run-off slave, for youngsters again felt and giggled over his colored person's hair. Then when there seemed to be a break in the questions from the small crowd, I tugged Mr. Finley forward, asking the Huckleberry man, "Are you spoken for at this current time, sir? Are you a married man?" Mr. Finley, beside me, did my blushing for me, I do believe.

"No, ma'am," he answered me quick, from beneath his straw hat.

Then he took his corncob pipe from his mouth and went on, happy for the new theme. "A body such as I couldn't ever keep a bride, nor be kept by one. Freedom, ma'am!" he boomed back to me, and to the others about us. "I needs my own dear freedom! Like others need air." He went song-like and showman-like for all of us.

Then I clung to Mr. Finley, and braved up again. "The right woman would do your soul well, Mr. Huckleberry," I answered that barefoot man in that tent. "Believe me, it surely would."

He listened to me, and then he crouched and paused. Then he spun about and he answered me fast, booming to the small crowd, "I'm as free as that mighty river! The big muddy! I can'st be civilized!"

Then we, the four of us, wandered on, as the Huckleberry Finn man boasted on to those we left behind, with me quite pleased with myself.

From there, though, my recollections of that evening fade and skip, or maybe they hide from me, knowing what's best for me. We must have wandered more, for by the time the four of us were ticketed and accounted for, and settled beneath the big top, the sun was already setting out over the mountains of the Bald Eagle Ridge.

That big show was just a two ringer, but oh my, that tent, from within or without, was still so large and looming, all beautifully lit with electric and kerosene lamps alike. One could have fit two of the Deacons' main barns in there, I'm sure.

And there were clowns and acrobats and tumblers, all moving and entertaining our happy audience to the music of their brass band, which played on into the night, never stopping, marking time for every act, even the animal ones with trained elephants, which knelt and curtsied for us with the trapeze people riding atop them. It seemed those circus folks all had their hands in one another's acts. And it was a pretty and a wonderful thing, seemingly balanced for the eyes, the ears and the hearts, for young and old alike.

Little Joshua and Emma loved the two moving shows, going on before us, laughing and clinging to Hank and I, and pointing to the devilish pranks of the clowns and the juggling jesters amongst the dazzling feats that silenced and stilled the large crowd. And we too, along with Joshua and Emma, held our breaths along with all else. Yes, the big show was all it was billed to be, until that one time when the ringmasters changed once more.

They must have rotated, you see, for it seemed as though there were four or five of those ringmasters working the two rings beneath that big top. To be short with this, it was when the ring before us got its third master when all fogged over and blurred to me, the sights and the sounds, those of the brass band and of the crowd as well. For I knew him, I did.

He was one of them. I was certain, down there before me, working his part of the show. It was monkeys in collars, with ladies so pretty and men so dashing. He was my fifth attacker. I reached to Hank Finley and touched him. Three of them dead, I thought to myself. One run off, for Gettysburg or Maryland, and now the fifth and final one, before my very eyes, boldly proclaiming his own name for that crowd, and I'll never forget it for the rest of my days.

"Rudolph Newbold Burr!" he sung out to all.

Then colorful midgets appeared, chased by lanky, cumbersome giants I recall from that blur of sights and sounds. Then I turned to Mr. Finley beside me, holding Joshua Deacon upon his lap. But his smile, too, was gone, as his gaze stayed fixed upon that man below us, turning wide-armed for the crowd, smiling in his waistcoat and top hat.

"Hank," I hushed out.

And he looked to me, and it must have been in my face or my eyes, for it was certainly in his. And then he answered a question I didn't ask.

"I know, Miss Clara," his kind mouth spoke. "It's him, ain't it? He's one of 'em, ain't he, because he's one of mine, too. I know it to be sure."

And just as quick, down below us, a tall, running man in a dark gray overcoat and cape suddenly appeared. Bumping into and toppling one of the giants from his stilts, that tall man seemed unaware of what he'd done.

Two of the scurrying midgets paused, looking confused. The ringmaster's back was turned to the approach of this man whom all else figured to be part of the show.

Then, when behind the ringmaster, the tall man's arm rose from beneath his dark cape, and I saw that glistening blade of his dagger.

The ringmaster turned. And screams filled the air as that man plunged that dagger deep into the ringmaster's face.

The man stepped back, as though to admire what he had done. The crowd surged about, nearly toppling us as the ringmaster stumbled, still on his feet, turning with his arms outstretched again, with that dagger still deep in his right eye, which then pushed out dark red blood, streaming down over his face.

Then another lone man ran out. Must have been a roustabout worker, for he tackled so at the cloaked, tall man, but the man flung him away as everything faded for me, into this odd silence, as her own hat came off—as he became a she—as her dark black hair fell about her wildly, as she went back after the ringmaster who fell to his knees before her.

More roustabouts appeared as the crowd, then wild, even at the far end, roared and screamed and panicked.

And that woman below fought on, while being overcome in a swirling mass of circus people as her dark self vanished away beneath those who subdued her.

And that vision alone is near all I can recall, save for looking to Hank Finley beside me as I clung to my Emma, as the circus goers about us lunged about like stricken cattle.

Hank Finley, himself, was holding tight to Joshua Deacon, with the stricken boy's face buried deep in Hank's own chest. Amongst the screaming and the hysteria, I couldn't hear Hank, for I couldn't hear anything. But I saw his mouth moving.

As though to some other time or place, I saw his mouth moving to his silent words.

"Oh, Annie," his mouth said. "Oh, you poor, poor thing, Annie."

CHAPTER 15

Homesickness now comes to my mind. Yes, from my recollection of that time it's homesickness, and homesickness' sad, staying pain.

I don't mean to say that I know what that feeling's made of, for I suppose it's the same and it's different for all who've known it, how it parades through the mind its own pictures and voices and sounds, thoughts of which a person's so used to, thoughts that fight with and push back the new so as the new ones can't settle themselves in, fitting and proper.

You see, Hank Finley did take me for his wife, and my Emma for his daughter, late that summer. And in the fall we moved away. And Emma and me, oh me oh my, how we missed the Deacon farm and the Deacon big house, the Deacons themselves, and Emma's little friends. We missed the dogs, I, that old bay, and all of us that Bald Eagle Mountain and the Loyalsock Creek. And yes, I do believe, no matter if young or old, one can long for the duties and the responsibilities that they've come to know as their very own lives. I felt it as a child, leaving my father's home, with my infant Emma, bound for the Deacons, then strangers. And oh, how I came to feel it again that autumn of 1890. And I found that feeling in my Scriptures, but I can't recall it just now. I wish I could.

I put this to paper now for homesickness still comes first and strongest and clearest, to my recollection of that time after that fourth and last murdering.

And Hank Finley was kind to us over it too.

"It's right hard leavin' your spot, Clara. I know so," he told me back then. We were on another walk, for we kept that habit.

"I know I'm being silly," I answered him, "but you've done it before, and so much more."

"Yes, I have, Clara, so I know your tears to be honest ones. But I also got to go back to a number of them places I missed on several occasions, and, ya know, I found them places not to be mine no more, for I found that life in them places went on with-out me, and that's a sad and true thing, but there is a good side."

"Then tell it to me," I asked of him.

"It's the new places where life will go on with you," he said as he wiped at my wet cheeks.

"It won't be the same."

"I know. It might well be better, though. Look what I found when I came here?" He smiled broad, then kissed at my forehead.

* * *

And as for that fourth murdering—Rudolph Newbold Burr—he passed away the following morning, under guard, up in the Williamsport hospital. They said, back then, that he never spoke a real word, leastways not anything that sounded like speech. They claimed he only moaned now and again, before slipping off into a long quiet, then into the heavens, I suppose.

Naturally, all had thoughts and opinions over it, the murderings that is, and of course over her, the "crazy woman" as she became known. This speculating and wondering surfaced in the churches as well, where the preachers took their own turns at reasoning with it. In our town it was mainly the Lutherans up on Broad Street and the Methodists near across the street from them, and of course my own house of worship out on Loyalsock Avenue. We Episcopalians were led and comforted by Reverend Ashhurst, who called upon us to pray for all involved, the victims, ourselves as accusers, and most righteously for that woman possessed, that nameless soul who murderously roamed our own little valley.

You see, she uttered few words herself, from the time of her capture, and across her imprisonment up in Williamsport's new stone jailhouse, up on Third Street. Also, none knew her, and many were given the chance, to provoke her, I guess, into talking, or into another rage, bound in her shackles behind those bars. Con-stables and community men alike were invited in from as far south as Harrisburg, as east as Scranton, as north as Elmira and as west as Lock Haven, to have good looks at her for themselves.

And those deemed "suspiciously close to the crime" were also brought in to give her audience, and opportunity. You see, even Mr. Finley and myself were put before her, as were those others. And we learned through Amos Reese that those others were many, being a stringing of every line of questioning that was pursued across those months since the faceless remains of Horace Wills turned up downriver in Muncy, or moreover, since those boys happened upon the rotting remains of Horace's still-saddled horse.

I feared for Hank and myself, for when our turns before her would come, for of course Hank knew her. You see, all selected were put before her one at a time, to the observations of her jailors, and of course with the Constable Keeler present. To my fear, I was to go before Hank. But when before her, with nothing but steel bars and thin air between us, she sat there, bound in her chains to a wooden chair, expressionless beneath her ragged black hair. And I knew the look, I did, that forever broken stare.

I spoke to her as instructed.

"My name is Clara Waltz, ma'am. Why did you do what you did?"

She never looked up, appearing even larger to me as I was so much closer to her then, than I was that night at the big show.

Nothing came of it, save more of my own praying over her. But she was tall to be sure, and even a touch pretty she could have been, in her own way, in her youth, or before her madness took her. Her eyes though looked like animal eyes, not wild though, or tame either, just pretty and real, but with near nothing behind them, such as Mrs. Snyder's, save without that ghostly soft haze.

I repeated my words, as whispered to do so. "My name is Clara Waltz, ma'am. Why did you do what you did?"

To my shaking words she stayed silent.

Hank's turn followed my own. He, though, would have some fifteen years in addition to the bars and the thin air between them, as I was kindly escorted just outside. I waited for several long minutes. Then a commotion stirred inside, and I feared up fast and terrible. Then there were more words said, clear and deliberate and not Hank's. Then laughter I thought, although I stayed fearful. Then Hank came out through them big heavy doors, alone and impossible to read, but at least he was out.

"Come, Clara. Let's go on home now," he said solemnly.

Then that big door opened wide behind us, and the one jailor leaned himself halfway out. He was young and odd looking, with a squirrel's face it seemed to me, with big teeth and gums that showed so, as he called out, "You ain't him, sir. No, you ain't him, not by the longest mile," as he laughingly closed himself back in.

"Ain't who, Hank?" I quietly asked.

"Home, Clara. Let's be on our way."

Then not a block away I asked him again, wishing to stay on it. "Who did that man mean by who you weren't?"

"Little Robbie, Clara," he answered me. "She called me 'Little Robbie' or leastways she said his name upon seeing me."

And I saw he was sad, so I left him alone with it forever after—in spite of learning different, years later.

* * *

And the *Gazette*, too, heralded the talk, either adding to it anew, or reflecting upon it, or just plain shoring it up for the curious. Amongst that, I mostly recall the discovery of her possible makeshift home while she was about our valley, and that too, back then, was only speculation.

It was a shanty on the opposite side of the river, in the trees just upriver from that collection of houses known as South Williamsport. Mainly, she, or some other large, silent-type woman had been seen about that crude structure, and of course a big wrench was found in there, with dried blood and hair and skin stuck to its ridge-like teeth. Joseph Logan's end, the law figured.

Those who had seen the keeper of that shanty were also paraded before the unknown Annie in her shackles, and they believed her to be her. She, of course, said nothing to their words.

In our Sunday services, the Reverend Ashhurst's last on it, to my knowing leastways, was of the sort of folks such as circus people can be.

"The sort that moves on," he declared, "roamers of a poor purpose, passing through we people of righteous roots, we people of law and order—never feeling answerable to our righteousness—parasites from the fruits of our own just rewards."

And he went on, he did, about how their judgments were declared for them here on Earth, and he kept his glance fast to me at that point of his. And then he asked fast, "For whom are we to understand?" And he was right about that. He surely was.

But we, Hank Finley and I, we did wonder over it anyway, and we talked of it when alone, in the safety of our courtship while walking again along the banks of the Loyalsock Creek.

"It seems to me, Clara," Hank told me, "that ole Annie joined up with the circus show in her own following sort of way."

"How so, Hank?"

"Well, a following through and through and driven with madness. She must of somehow gotten away, I reckon, free of that asylum place, with a single mind bent for returning the evil which was visited upon her and her little boy."

"I see. Maybe that's so," I answered him. "Maybe she just couldn't wait for the Judgement."

"As I couldn't either, at least for one of 'em?" he asked me without looking to me.

"I'm praying for you, Hank, for that. Let's not talk of it."

"I hope He listens to you," he quietly said, looking out over the tumbling water of the creek.

"He does, Hank. But why Joseph Logan? He couldn't have been one of hers, for all of mine are dead, save for Stacy Kremer who's run off they say. That makes only three of hers dealt with so cruelly. Two others may still be at large while she was busy at killing Joseph, whom she couldn't have known."

"Crazed, Miss Clara. But not dumb nor ignorant," he figured and told me. "She could read and write right well. I knew of her to pick up a newspaper time and again. And if you recall, that Joseph feller didn't have kind words for Charlie's killer in the *Gazette*. She could'a read it, I'll wager, Clara, and she were crazed, ya know."

Then Hank got thoughtful on that walk of ours along the Loyalsock. "And I'd wager she got her other two before she come up this way, Miss Clara, after these others. I'd bet she did."

"Why do you think that?" I asked him, while being most evil myself, hoping that it might have been so.

"She didn't hide herself about this last one, Clara. Not a'tall. Like she was done with it at last, marching herself out there that night for all to see."

And that figured, it did. It did make sense to me.

But Hank stopped those thoughts with, "Madness to be sure, Clara. But a madness of purpose it must'a been. Perhaps a purpose at last satisfied."

And I supposed he was right over that, for she was clever enough to not get caught with her acts before that last one.

In reflection now, all these years after, I suppose things often end as they begin, with just small parts of those same things just trying to stay alive. Not but two weeks after Rudolph Newbold Burr's death, of which I already told enough of, came the slow end of the unknown one, Annie Payne.

Word had it that she fell fast in her health, the health of her body, that is. They said that she never took to her meals up there in that stone jail. A little water now and again, but that was all, and none ever saw her take it either. It just turned up gone. Well, it was pneumonia that eventually took her, and it took her fast once it had her. The authorities took her far away to lay her to rest, leastways that's one story. Another claimed she was buried before a dawn in the hills west of Lycoming Creek.

That wouldn't spoil mine and Mr. Finley's nuptials though, for we said them to Reverend Ashhurst near two months later, in the first week of September. And it was a small gathering, it was, with the Deacons allowing their parlor for us and our few guests. Elizabeth did us well, decorating her parlor with her own mums from her eastside garden. They were mainly those rusty-colored ones, all tied up in pretty bows and hung so nicely about the room.

Hank and I, we wore the very clothes we wore to serve the Deacons' anniversary gala earlier that summer. But I did see to a proper bustle though, after quietly sharing my earlier unfitfulness with Mrs. Deacon, who saw me all proper to a fashionable undercarriage.

As for our vows, Reverend Ashhurst moved us through them quick, and at one point I heard the front doors open from the verandah, and oh how I wished it so in my heart, but it just wasn't to be. Instead, the farmhand, Sam the boy, stumbled in. As I related earlier, so far back in this recollection, my own father would never speak to me again. Not ever.

* * *

Oh me oh my, how I do hate so to finish this recollection that I began last fall, with all the leaves turning so pretty outside and such. But outside my lonely windows a new spring is upon me, with the bushes and the trees slowly greening, with me here penciling away at this thing, wishing, I suppose, to not become another poor old Mrs. Snyder, having to leave behind photographs as the story of my husband and I. But I must pencil on for the reason that I began to last fall.

Well, next came the homesickness of course, for we moved away, we did, to Scranton, where Hank took work with the railroad over there in coal country. As he told me early on, he kept his brotherhood dues paid up, thus he had no trouble finding work for good wages.

Rebecca had her baby long prior to our leaving. James Wilson Snyder III they named him. Then poor old Mrs. Snyder died, not long after we got to Scranton. Elizabeth wrote me often, you see, and told me of it. We'd correspond for a number of years we would, which is how I also learned of Stacy Kremer's returning home to his farm, and with a wife from wherever it was he had gone off to. I was happy for him, after praying over it some.

And then we moved again, four years later, but not before my giving birth to my third child, whom we named Todd, Todd Finley, our so serious one. And not before Hank's and I's own settling into our wedded lives together. Oh how we shared such times and caring. Proverbs says it best, and it was us, it was. In 5:15, "Drink water out of your own cistern, and tricklings out of the mist of your own well." And from 5:18 and beyond: "Let your water source prove to be blessed, and rejoice with the wife of your youth, a loveable hind and a charming mountain goat. Let her own breasts intoxicate you. With her love may you be in ecstasy constantly."

Oh me oh my, we tugged and tussled with one another too, mind you. Sometimes our house wasn't big enough for the both of us, but our loving fellowship for one another never strayed off, never for long, especially for whom he truly was, for on occasion we'd hear of stories concerning his possible fugitive doings and whereabouts. Once I even got to listen in on educated men talking of that boy in that book, of his faithlessness in his choosing "his river god" to lead him. So I tried it out and thought of my Hank in that way, but I couldn't see it. And as I tell of this now, I can't rightly say if this is a story of him, or the story of me. Perhaps it is ours, of the both of us, with how our lives did come to be braided together in our caring for each other. I suppose, after all, that it was me who was in such need of the extra god, one here on Earth, with justice and love for whom I was as a mere foolish girl, and more then, as a damaged woman beyond.

* * *

Oh, how things and times have changed since Hank Finley and I first happened upon one another back then. How they have indeed. Why it's right common nowadays for near all to have a bathing tub built right into their family's own home. In towns, most decent folks in decent houses can call upon hot water at the turn of a tap. Some even have these new washing machines to see them through their washing. I could go on and on, but I won't, for I see what I'm doing, and I must move on.

And how it truly pains me to end this, for it's like closing him to his grave once more, it is. But I must, and I shall.

We stayed on in Scranton for four years, where Todd came into our lives there, our serious child as I told of before. Then railroading of the sort that Hank preferred took us up into New York State, to the little city of Binghamton, where we bought another nice little house. Hank was prudent and thrifty with his money, you see. I learned this just after our marriage, and I was pleased for I was of the same sort. And it was there, in Binghamton, where I gave birth to our second son, little Johnny.

I turned thirty-nine that year, and we were thankful all were safe. By then Todd was already six, and my first, my little survivor, my Emma, was all of a young woman at twenty-one. I wrote to Elizabeth Deacon over it, and that letter would prove to be our final correspondence. No, I'd never hear from her again, nor anything of any of the Deacons, or of their friends or farm or of that town that was once our home.

Baby Johnny became our rambunctious one, he did, always into it and with a ready grin at that. Oh, he was a lively one, he was. Then near two years later my Emma married off, into a good Binghamton family, to Jason Bower, a banking man. Emma, by then, was nearly finished with her studies at the local Normal School for Girls, and would become a schoolteacher herself. We, and most especially myself, were so proud of her. And it was about that time, that she asked me who her real father was. We were alone, walking together. I told her, and I told her why I believed this. And her eyes went glassy upon learning that her "Poppa Hank" had always known. She asked if it pained him, and I told her no. You see, I too once asked him the same question, and he eased me true, telling me the world was a better place with Emma in it. And as we walked, I told her this. She smiled and cried, then I did too.

Then we made our last move, we did, in 1906, leaving Emma behind to her new family, with tears of my own, I might add.

We moved, believe it or not, over and across our new state's southern tier, to Elmira, New York, for Hank's last years of his railroading. And it's a nice little city, and the very city where that famous Samuel Clemons was still residing, outside of town on a farm somewhere in those surrounding pretty hills. We even saw him once, but at a distance. And he was in one of his famous white suits to boot, but he was moving awfully slow for he was near his own end, he was. Hank figured the whole business of our own living so near to him right funny indeed, figuring the courses of everyone's lives, known and unknown.

Well, the boys, then, they grew like weeds, and stayed true to themselves too, with Todd so right and quiet and proper, and with little Johnny, the lively one, always wet or dirty or hungry or just stung by bees or something. Johnny, at thirteen or so, also took on his father's big bobbing Adam's apple. And it was, and still is, so pretty to me today. Todd, he favored me for sure. And I could see a lot of Emma in him as well, what wasn't of her true father's, of course.

Then in 1915, at twenty-one, Todd quietly married himself off to a local girl here, Margaret Wellington. And he found good work over in Corning at the big glass factory. He's still there, these years and a large sorrow later. Then in 1917, with me at fifty-five, and Hank still with his health at seventy-five, little Johnny got called off to the Great War over in Europe.

Hank, he pained in silence over it, the whole time. As for me I took to my Scriptures, and prayed over him daily. Johnny's letters came in surges, between stretches of nothing, which scared us. And they were painful things in that forever-childish script of his, which told us of endless trenches of mud and of the dead, and of the stench of the fallen horses which weren't retrieved, and of having to live within those terrible gas masks over their faces. Yes, times had changed, they had.

And of course there was Johnny's homecoming, that so happy, so sad day of his safe return to us. You see, in one of his letters, he shared with his father his sorrows over killing. I foolishly shared it with our one neighbor lady, Mrs. Kelly, a brassy thing, always after her brood of kids. I liked her, I still do, but as it came to be, she shared my sad news with one or more of those children of hers. Well, when Johnny came into sight upon our street, dressed in his uniform and walking alone, which was how he wished to return, the little children of the street screamed and cried, and ran and hid, struck with horror at the sight of the killer. I wept for him, I did. He came home whole of body, but something else was gone and gone for good.

* * *

Now it's 1922 as I write these very words, and the changing keeps coming. My dear and kind old Hank, he died back in the late fall of 1920, just two months past our thirtieth wedding anniversary, which was about a year and a half ago. And that was twelve years after the passing of Samuel Clemons himself, and three years after a series of strokes took old man Tom Sawyer to his own great beyond, of which I have to add a touch of here, for it may be of interest.

You see, back when our Johnny was off to the Great War, the passing of that Tom Sawyer prompted the *Harper's* magazine people to run off a search for his long lost, fabled, boyhood companion. Well, some dozen or so old buggers stepped forward and staked claims to being him, but nothing was proven of course. The article was just fun for all around, I suppose. I myself came upon it spread across Hank's lap as I found him napping upon my return from my Sunday services back in that October of 1917.

Then I was took back again, just prior to the Christmas season of that same year, with this newer magazine's—*The Saturday Evening Post*—own take on the subject. Their feature, though, asked for no volunteers as their writer sought out and reviewed the most colorful of the tales about. This writer claimed he came across nearly sixty in all, of which he put down the most interesting dozen or so. One, though, caught me. It was originally related by a Delaware man, a sound country lawyer, who had this great uncle who once entertained the lawyer's family with this remembrance of his own of nearly thirty years before, when the great uncle labored as a jailor as a young man. The lawyer couldn't truthfully recall where, Ohio or Pennsylvania he guessed. But he could recall this insane woman from the tale, a murderous woman who said so little of so little sense as possible collaborators were paraded before her cell, one at a time. But to the entrance of one lone man she up and startled all about her cell, saying out, "Huck Finn," to none in particular and with an odd smile aimed at the air, as though prompted by the entrance of that man. Nothing else moved her though, so the quiet man was excused, the lawyer's second uncle claimed. Then the writer moved his story on.

* * *

And my Hank, his dear old soul, he passed away in his sleep nearly three years later, and I of course arose to it in the morning, and knew it first off. I stayed with him though, I did, for he did turn out to be my savior of a sort. And not that it matters any, but we did lay him to rest, the children and I, not but a hundred yards or so from Samuel Clemons' own resting. And oh me oh my, I did love my Mr. Hank Finley, I did, as I still do now as I write these thoughts and recollections.

My Emma, she's forty-three now, and still over in Binghamton with her husband, Jason, and their near-grown brood of four. Emma's back to her school teaching at their grammar school too, and her daughters, May and Jilly, they do write to me often and I do so enjoy them.

Todd, he's twenty-eight, and remarried. You see, Margaret, she died on him in the struggle of her second childbirth, oh, four years ago just about. Her baby survived and Todd named him William. So with baby Billy and JoAnne, their first, he went on and married Margaret's cousin, Marintha, another Wellington, and the two now have three youngsters all together.

You see, Marintha was a touch like I as a child, for she brought a child of her own into their marriage. Todd, though, could see the goodness in her, just as his own dear father could see mine in me, I suppose.

Johnny's twenty-two now, and yet to be married. I think, though, that he may be falling in love with a young woman, but he's keeping it from me for now. Like that logger's wife was, Mrs. Mary Barclay, this girl's dark haired and dark eyed, and kind of spooky. Johnny also bought a little bit of a farm out near Horseheads two and half years ago. Hank liened the house on the loan for him just months before he passed away. We were both happy that he chose farming, never knowing that Emma's stories of the Deacons' farm, told to him over and again when he was so little, would stay within him. I suppose the war contributed some as well. No matter, his smile and his laugh are no longer as ready, nor as often, but they are returning, I do believe. Maybe it's that young girl he's hiding. But he cares for me he does, and he looks in on me more than I need here about my quiet house.

And as for me, I'm sixty-one years old now, and in good, sturdy health. I may live on ten or twenty years, or I may be called home in three or four, but that's no matter for this tale of recollection that I'm finally putting down. For it's truly time that I gather it all up and put the pages in proper order, to tuck it all neatly away in some box and label upon it "For You, Children," for one of them to find one day, as they'll have to go through my things after my passing to my own just rewards. And then, whenever, they'll at least wonder over all of this—this blessing, or curse, from their mother.

You see, the children, not a one of them, ever knew how their dear old father came to meet up with their mother, to love one another so, save his being a farmhand at the farm where I labored as that same farm's house-girl. Hank wouldn't have any of it. Well, he's gone now and it's just me and them, and I do so love them, them and their spouses, and their own dear children. And I still love my Hank Finley too, which is why I had to do this.

So now they have it, and all of it is true, this small harvest of pretty days. For their loving, quiet old man of a father was indeed a sufferer as a child, a boy born as Henry Jacob Finn. And he was a killer too, and he was, indeed, that boy to be fabled so, that runaway boy, cast near forever after, until this remembrance, as that lost and wandering boy—who came home to me.

Did you enjoy this book?
Visit ForemostPress.com to share
your comments or a review.
And discover more fun stuff.

2/08

Printed in the United States
201097BV00011B/27/A